The Search for Noah's Ark

STEVE BOGGESS

THE SEARCH FOR NOAH'S ARK

TATE PUBLISHING & *Enterprises*

Published by Tate Publishing & Enterprises, LLC
127 E. Trade Center Terrace | Mustang, Oklahoma 73064 USA
1.888.361.9473 | www.tatepublishing.com

Tate Publishing is committed to excellence in the publishing industry. The company reflects the philosophy established by the founders, based on Psalm 68:11,
"The Lord gave the word and great was the company of those who published it."

Cover design by Tyler Evans
Interior design by Cole Roberts

Published in the United States of America

ISBN: 978-1-60799-077-2
1. Fiction / Christian / Historical
09.08.12

Dedication

I'd like to dedicate this book to Barb Stockton and Marv Essary. Barb started me on the road to internet writing while I was doing a tour of duty in Iraq. My first article was on the Abu Ghraib soldier/prisoner scandal. I still do not believe one can judge how the United States Army really operates on the actions of a handful of idiotic, undisciplined soldiers.

Marv Essary, for believing in me on the word of Barbara alone, and he has worked with me over the course of the past five years. I am still going strong in writing internet articles on politics and current events.

I also wish to thank a very good friend of mine, Michelle Cline, who lives in Gig Harbor, Washington. I let her read the first few pages of this book while it was still a manuscript and she told me that to her it looked like a really good read.

I would like to say a special *thank you* to Ryan Tate, president and CEO of Tate Publishing, and to Vince Conn, my conceptual editor, who, in my opinion, has made me a better writer. He let me know that after the final edits and recommended corrections were done, that when I sent them back to him that that would be the finished product before being published to a nationwide audience. That made me think long and hard about how I wanted my book to read. And also to Tyler Evans, who designed the book cover. His creative thoughts and work on this had everything to do with the contents of my book and because of this, his first two ideas were brilliant and I chose the book cover the reader is now holding. I also want to thank Curtis Winkle, my senior editor at Tate and Dave Dolphin, director of Book Production and to Rachael Sweeden, who is Director of Operations. Special thanks also go to Donna Chumley, who sent me the writing contract for Tate. Even though that at the time I sent her an uncompleted 40 page manuscript, she and Tate still took a chance on me. A thank you also goes out to Melissa Madole, Associate Director of Multimedia.

I also want to thank my first cousin Gerald Anthony George (Tony to the rest of the family), who proof read the completed manuscript and gave me his "thumbs up" on how it read. I thank my first cousin, Kelly George, who is married to Tony, for her support on all of this and for both of them keeping me in their prayers.

I also want to thank Pastor Dave and Becky Sinclair of Temple Baptist Church in South Charleston, West Virginia. Both of them continued to encourage me to hold fast to both my faith in things unseen and my dreams as well. The book the reader is holding is one of those dreams. I want to thank the church congregation as well. Even though we're a small country church, we're also family.

I thank my aunt Sue Frye who told me stories of how I loved to read the newspaper when I was a child, and even though I couldn't understand the subject or content of what I was reading, I could pronounce the big words. Thanks to my aunt, Janet Boggess, who kept me on my toes and on the "straight and narrow" when it came to finishing this book. She also showed me all of the articles I had written for the conservative online newsmagazine I write for that she had collected, and still collects when I visited the family the first time two years ago. I did not know she was doing that. I moved back to my home state of West Virginia after being gone for 20 years and at that time, I only had six months left to finish the manuscript and I still wasn't much farther along than the previously mentioned 40 pages, but this was also due to some personal issues as well. Thank you to my uncle Emory Boggess, who wished me "the best" in both writing this book and also the hoped for success after the publication. Thanks also to Connie and Jimmy Pritt and family for just being there. All of our hearts go out to them for their loss just a few months ago.

Lastly, I also want to dedicate this book to me. It's my first of hopefully many more to come. This book started as an idea in 2005 when I was still stationed in Wiesbaden, Germany, as previously mentioned, where I was living in the Hainerberg Housing area. Although it started out as an idea, it transformed into a dream and from there, slowly morphed into the reality it now is.

I thank God for all the blessings He has given me since I got out of the United States Army and all the rest to come.

—*Steve Boggess*
February 13, 2009
Sissonville, West Virginia

Preface

I wrote this book because I became discouraged at how often the Bible, the holy Word of God, has been attacked over the years by certain authors, ideologues, Hollywood movies, actors, singers, and all those who call themselves entertainers. I will say outright that I am a God-fearing, Christian man, and that does not make me perfect in any way, shape, or form. It merely makes me forgiven by the saving grace of Jesus Christ. I am still very much a human man with all the flaws that come with being born into sin. I have my hang-ups, character flaws, issues, and everything else that accompanies man's sinful nature.

I got the idea for this book when I was an active-duty United States Army Soldier stationed at Wiesbaden Army Airfield in Wiesbaden, Germany. Just so everyone knows, because it usually comes up when someone asks, "What unit were you in?" I was assigned to the 421st Medical Detachment on the airfield, but before that, I was also assigned to the 557th Ground Ambulance Company (GA) just up the street from the 421st. I went to war with the 557th in Iraq in 2004. I was a sergeant. I was also stationed in Germany from 2001–2006.

I also got the idea from watching a documentary on Dan Brown's number-one bestseller, *The DaVinci Code.* I read this book from cover to cover and thought it was an excellent story, and I also saw the movie. There is a part in the movie where English actor Sir Ian McKellen's character Sir Leigh Teabing, who is an English historian, attempts to "prove" to Tom Hanks' character, Harvard symbologist Robert Langdon, and also to French actress Audrey Tatou's character Sophie Neveu that Jesus Christ was not the son of God by a showing a painting of DaVinci's *The Last Supper.* Sir Leigh attempts to show how it was not the beloved disciple John sitting next to Jesus, but the Catholic church-smeared woman, Mary Magdelene.

I thought to myself, *Wouldn't it be wonderful if someone, anyone, would write a book not only defending Jesus' divinity, but also laying to rest the other opinions that deny it as well.* But opinions are just that, opinions. I can't change what anyone else says, thinks, or believes, but I can put my own opinion out there that I do believe that Jesus was and is the one and only Son of the living God.

In telling a story about the flood, there are two accepted ones: the biblical story, albeit, not really believed by a majority of those who don't believe anything the Bible has to say. And then there is the epic of Gilgamesh. Although the two stories parallel each other very loosely, the reader can make up his or her own mind.

On the Web site Creation.com, author Jonathan Sarfati wrote an article about this in March 2004. In it, he writes about both the Genesis flood and the epic of Gilgamesh and goes on to compare the two. He begins his article by quoting the Scottish physician James Hutton (1726–1797) who, according to Mr. Sarfati, was quoted as saying, "The past history of our globe must be explained by what can be seen to be happening now. No powers are to be employed that are not natural to the globe, no action to be admitted except those of which we know the principle." Dr. Hutton declared this in 1785 before he looked at the evidence.

Jonathan Sarfati is a creationist author, and his writings on creationism have attracted attention from opponents and supporters alike. He works for Creation Ministries International, which is a non-profit Christian apologetics ministry, specializing in young-earth creationism.

According to Sarfati, this was not a refutation of biblical teaching of creation and the flood but a dogmatic refusal to consider them as even possible explanations.

Then I happened to watch a documentary on the Discovery Channel about Noah's Ark. The title of the piece, *Noah's Ark: The True Story,* shows the ark story from every angle but that of the Bible. The piece also mentioned the Sumerian *Epic of Gilgamesh.* This story was first unearthed in 1853 by British archeologist Sir Austen Henry Layard when he was excavating the palace library in the ancient Assyrian capital of Nineveh. Among their finds were a series of twelve tablets of a great epic, or story. These tablets dated from about 650 b.c., but the poem inscribed therein was much older. The hero in this epic, Gilgamesh, according to the Sumerian king list, was a king of the first dynasty of Uruk who reigned for 126 years. In the epic of Gilgamesh, the hero is two-thirds divine and one-third mortal, and he has enormous intelligence and strength but also oppresses his people. The people then call upon the gods and, more specifically, the "sky god, Anu," who is the chief god of the city. He makes a wild man called Enkidu whose own strength rivals that of

Gilgamesh. They fight, but neither can win. The contest ends in mutual respect for one another.

The two friends set off on adventures together, but the sky gods eventually kill Enkidu, which throws Gilgamesh into a grievous period of mourning. Gilgamesh then realizes he too will eventually die, and he learns of one man who did become immortal. That person is called Utnapishtim, who is a survivor of a global flood. Utnapishtim's story is told on the eleventh tablet of the Gilgamesh epic.

In the biblical story, God commands Noah to build the ark as the LORD has seen fit to destroy all mankind due to their absolute wickedness. God also tells Noah that he is sorry that he created man. So Noah begins to build the ark when he was six hundred years old. After the ark is completed, Noah and his family are the only ones, besides the animals that God brought to him to stow on the ark, to survive.

According to Mr. Sarfati's article, disbelief in the Genesis flood has become so entrenched that even many ostensibly Christian colleges don't teach it. However, Jesus himself taught that the flood was real history—just as real as his future second coming when he said in the book of Luke 17:26–27: "Just as it was in the days of Noah, so also shall it be in the days of the Son of Man. People were eating, drinking, marrying and being given in marriage up to the day Noah entered the Ark. Then the flood came and destroyed them all."

I do believe the Bible is the eternal Word of God and that Jesus is his resurrected Son. I believe the Bible was written according to divine revelation, and it is not to be added to or anything removed from. It is everlasting in its teachings and, like its author, God, does not change at all over time.[1]

—*Steve Boggess*
February 13, 2009
Sissonville, West Virginia

Introduction

The LORD saw how great man's wickedness on the earth had become, and that every inclination of the thoughts of his heart was only evil all the time. The LORD was grieved that he had made man on the earth, and his heart was filled with pain.

So the LORD said, "I will wipe mankind, whom I have created, from the face of the earth—men and animals, and creatures that move along the ground, and birds of the air—for I am grieved that I have made them."

But Noah found favor in the eyes of the LORD.

This is the account of Noah.

Noah was a righteous man, blameless among the people of his time, and he walked with God. Noah had three sons; Shem, Ham, and Japheth.

Now the earth was corrupt in God's sight and was full of violence. God saw how corrupt the earth had become, for all the people on the earth had corrupted their ways. So God said to Noah, "I am going to put an end to all people, for the earth is filled with violence because of them. I am surely going to destroy both them and the earth.

So make yourself an Ark of cypress wood; make rooms in it and coat it with pitch inside and out. This is how you are to build it; the ark is to be four hundred and fifty feet long, seventy-five feet wide, and forty-five feet high. Make a roof for it and finish the ark to within eighteen inches of the top. Put a door in the side of the ark and make lower, middle, and upper decks. I am going to bring flood waters on the earth to destroy all life under the heavens, every creature that has the breath of life in it. Everything on earth will perish.

But I will establish my covenant with you, and you will enter the ark—you and your sons and your wife and your sons' wives with you. You are to bring into the ark two of all living creatures, male and female, to keep them alive with you. Two of every kind of bird, of every kind of animal, and of every kind of creature that moves along the ground will come to you to be kept alive. You are to take every kind of food that is to be eaten and store it away as food for you and for them.

Noah did everything just as God commanded.

Genesis 6:5–22

ALLEGED EYE WITNESS ACCOUNTS OF NOAH'S

275 b.c. Berossus, a Chaldean priest and historian. He was quoted by Lucius Cornelius Alexander (1st Century b.c.), a Greek scholar who was enslaved by the Romans and had extensive knowledge. And by Flavius Josephus (a.d. 37–101), a Jewish historian. Berossus' account is a version of the Babylonian flood account when he notes that, "The Ark is grounded in Armenia and some part still remains in the mountains of Gordyaeans in Armenia, and some get pitch from the ship by scraping off, and use it for amulets."

50 a.d. Josephus, who was Jewish by birth, but loyal to the Roman Empire. He was a man of great intellect and a contemporary of the Apostle Paul. He was also the official historian of the Jews for the Roman Empire and he had access to all the archives and libraries of his day. He mentions the remains of Noah's Ark three times and all can be found in his work, Antiquities of the Jews, a history of the Jewish people, beginning with the creation of Adam and Eve.

315–403 a.d. The bishop of Salamis, Epiphanius. He was born into a Jewish family in the small settlement of Besanduk, Judea. He converted to Christianity and lived as a monk in Egypt. On two occasions he mentions that the Ark landed in the mountains of Gordians. He maintains that the remains of the Ark and that if one looks diligently, the alter of Noah can still be seen.

1254 a.d. Haithon, the Armenian king and son of Constantine, Lord of Baberon, said of Noah's Ark, "In Armenia there is a very high mountain-the highest in existence-and its name is Ararat. On that mountain, Noah's Ark landed after the flood. No one can climb this mountain because of the great quantity of snow on it in winter and summer. But at the summit, a great black object is always visible, the Ark of Noah."

13th Century a.d. Marco Polo, the Venetian trader and explorer who gained fame for his world wide travels, was informed by the villagers who lived in the foothills of Mount Ararat that Noah's Ark still rests upon its summit.

1829. Dr. Friedrich Parrot, a Baltic German naturalist and traveler, led a scientific mountaineering expedition up Mount Ararat. His party reached the summit on September 27, 1829. Parrot glacier is named for him. Years later, an 1840 earthquake shook the mountain and the Ahora Gorge was formed.

1883. Turkish Commission. In the summer of 1883, a massive earthquake rocked the mountain and destroyed a number of villages. Turkish officials and a British attaché went to investigate the amount of damage to the area and reportedly, came upon a "huge boat like structure jutting out from an overhanging glacier." The team reportedly entered the structure but terminated any further investigation for fear the glacier might fall on them.

1908. George Hagopian, an Armenian boy, climbed the mountain with his uncle and supposedly reached the Ark. George was about ten years old at the time. He climbed to the top of the Ark and described it as "a flat bottomed petrified barge without nails and it had many windows on top. Each big enough for a cow to walk through." Two years later, he again visited the Ark. George passed away in 1972.

1936. Hardwicke Knight, who was a young archeologist, made an accidental discovery in the glacial ice at the 14, 000 levels on the northern slopes and was within a few yards of the Ahora Gorge. He discovered "huge timbers" extending out of the glacial ice. Although he did not consider this find to have anything to do with the Ark, in depths study of those timbers convinced him they may have come from it.

1917/1942. United States Navy Machinist Mate Ray Lubeck. Claims to have seen a silent film of fifty Russian soldiers marching past Noah's Ark near the top of Mount Ararat. Ray was a machinist mate 1st Class on Midway Island in 1942. In order to keep morale up, the Navy, Marine Corp and Air Force would show movies on occasion. One film clip that lasted anywhere from thirty seconds to two minutes showed those same Russian soldiers marching past the Ark. The film was black and white, silent, and had a voice-over narrator describing the events unfolding on screen.

1917/1970. Russian Armais Arutunoff, Dave DuMaer photos of a box like object on Mount Ararat on a cliff or a ledge.

1918. United States Air Force Officer Guillford claimed to have seen a box like structure in ice on the fourteen thousand foot level of Mount Ararat.

1920. Russian Army Major Jasper Maskelyn claims to have seen the Ark on Mount Ararat.

1935–1941. American Bertha Davis photos of a box like structure on Mount Ararat.

1940–1941. Australian "Aussie" R. Taylor/Nice/Tibbets photos of Noah's Ark in a basin next to hogback ridge.

1943. United States Army Sergeant Ed Davis who was stationed in Hamadan, Iran, became friends with some local Kurdish tribesmen who told him of the Ark being on the mountain. The Ark and the items from it were considered holy relics and were kept from outsiders. However, Davis' friendship with the Kurdish chief made him the exception. They showed him items from the Ark, including a cage door, latches and shepherds' staff. All the wooden items were described as petrified. The tribal leader, Abas-Abas and seven of his sons led Davis up the northeast side of Mount Ararat, but bad weather prevented them from getting any closer than a half mile from the Ark. According to Davis, he did see it, but it was also broken into three or four pieces and he saw two. The nearer piece had at least three floors. Abas-Abas told Davis that the top floor was the living space for Noah and his family and that the Ark's door was hinged at the top and that the Ark was built using wooden pegs.

1943. United States Air Corp Sergeant Vince Will was with the 3356 Signal Installation Battalion attached to the Army Air Force and he was also co-pilot of a C-47 cargo plane that flew over Mount Ararat. He describes the Ark as resting on a ledge with a large drop off. Three floors were seen with prominent central alley way through a hole on its side.

1946. Charlie McCallen claimed to have seen a newsreel that contained footage of Noah's Ark sometime between July 4, 1946 and late 1947 in a Jackson, Tennessee movie theater. He claims the time of footage was between 30–60 seconds. Charlie was 100% sure the Ark was manmade and was also sure the structure was Noah's Ark. He described the structure as being square shaped and that the front and top were broken which allowed many rooms to be viewed from both above and in the end of the Ark. The rooms looked almost square. There were two-three levels and the Ark was charcoal black in color.

1948. Shukru Arsena, who was a sixty-nine year old Kurdish farmer who owned land in the Eastern Turkey frontier district, told his story to the Associated Press in 1948. Early in September, another Kurdish farmer named Reshit was about two-thirds of the way up the 16,969 foot peak when he came upon an object he had never seen before, even though he had been on the mountain several times. He moved around and climbed higher to get a better look at it. Reshit recalls the prow of a ship protruding into a canyon from which tons of ice and snow had been melting for months. The prow of the ship was almost entirely revealed, but the rest of it was still covered. The contour of the earth he said indicated the invisible part of the ship was shaped like a ship and that the prow was about the size of a house. He claimed he climbed down to it and tried to take a sample from it with his dagger, but it was so hard it would not break. He insisted it was not a rock formation and that he knew a ship when he saw one.

1953–1955. William Todd, who at the age of 27 was a photographers mate chief who joined the United States Navy on June 24, 1944 and retired in 1965 after 21 years of service. The Navy Hydrographic Office from Washington D.C. And the Army Map Service combined with the Turkish Air Force to give the first working accurate map of the country of Turkey. Mr. Todd claims that he was assigned to U.S. Navy unit V.J. 61, which was attached to the Turkish Air Force in both Ismir and Diyarbakir. His unit was flying the U.S. Naval AJ2-P photographic configured Savage aircraft. From 1951–1955 the Navy was in charge of mapping the entire nation of Turkey. One afternoon, an anomaly was spotted while they were descending into Diyarbakir. They decided to turn around and investigate it. They flew to the altitudes of between 14,500–16,000 feet when a structure was spotted lying on a shelf protruding from ice and snow. They witnessed the structure from 2,000 feet. The object was huge and was filled with ice and snow. He shot one roll of aerial film four hundred feet long by nine inches wide and after processing the film and using the correct formulaic scale, determined the structure to be seventy five feet wide by forty five feet high. The other eyewitnesses in Mr. Todd's group were Joe Gorsky, a retired U.S. Naval pilot and commander of Russian descent, and Ensign Glacow.

1969–1970. Lieutenant Colonel Walter Hunter saw two photos of what was allegedly Noah's Ark and were in the possession of men working in Base Operations at Beale Air Force Base in California. He stated that an object in the photos looked like a boat which was encased in a glacier. He said he did not know who took the photos but were probably taken from a U-2 spy air craft. The object, he said, looked to be about 450 feet long and was pointed on both ends. He describes the viewing of the photos a "passing thing" as he was about to file his flight plan.

1992–1993. Rolando Reyna and his father were watching KMEX, a Mexico City television station during a Saturday night news program which showed a Turkish military film with a green tint to it. The shaky film which was taken from a helicopter and lasting 35–45 seconds showed a three deck structure sticking approximately 15 feet out of the ice with long broken timbers lying below it in the snow. He also stated that there were three other helicopters hovering over it to determine the entire width of the object. The object was filmed on the north side of Mount Ararat.

Chapter 1

The phone on Dr. Ian James's desk rang. It rang as he was doing some online research on Rameses, one of the kings of ancient Egypt. He had read an article on the king that was written by his old friend Dr. Abu Nadir-Mustafa, who had written an article about the king during the time of the plagues on Egypt because he had refused to let the Israelites free from bondage and out of Egypt when Moses told him it was time and because the God of Israel said so. He had been out of touch with his friend for some time due to busy schedules and both their careers had taken different paths. He had taken the tenure at the University of Oregon to teach the ancient Egyptian studies course. He was paid a king's ransom do so.

"Hello?" the professor said as he spoke into the phone.

"Dr. James, someone named Dr. Mustafa is on line two for you. He says it's urgent."

"Dr. Mustafa?" Dr. James thought to himself, *What makes him call me here in the States? Must be important for him to do that.* He remembered how tight-fisted his old friend used to be when it came to money. Abu hated to spend money on anything unless he could find a valid reason to do so. He was always giving Ian free advice on how to save his money, whether he wanted it or not. Abu's father had been a banker by trade, and while Abu was born with the proverbial silver spoon in his mouth, his father taught him that even though one is born into privilege, you can't take it with you when you die, and you must be very wise in how you save your money. His father often said that just because you have money doesn't mean you must spend it. Ian also remembered the saying Abu's father taught him that always seemed so geeky when Abu would say it to Ian; "You're always nifty when you're thrifty."

"Put him through, Linda," James said into the phone's intercom. "Hello?"

"Dr. James, it's Dr. Mustafa, how are you my old friend? I bet you're wondering why I am calling you, long distance no doubt."

"Well that thought did cross my mind, Abu. So how is everything going on your end? Still digging all of ancient Egypt up? Still bothering the pharaohs in their mortal slumber?"

"Ian, something came up during the Ramses dig. Something no one would have even expected in a lifetime. It's of great urgency that I see you; I am calling you on my office phone, instead of my cell. I fear that if I had called you from my cell, there would be many more ears other than yours that would be listening. That cannot happen."

"Calm down, Abu. I'm sure that whatever it is can be explained. My God, you sound as if you've seen a ghost."

"No, not a ghost, Ian, but something that just shouldn't

be on the wall inside a pharaoh's tomb, something I would have never expected to see."

"Abu, whatever it is, like I said, I'm sure it can be explained. What is it, the transcript one of the scribes left of Ramses Bible class, for laughing crying out loud?"

"Ian, it's funny you should mention the Bible."

Dr. Mustafa got a rather curious look on his face at the mention of the word Bible in the same sentence as the name of one of the most famous pharaohs in all of Egypt and the Bible.

Dr. Mustafa had been called to the tomb because of some significant finding there. This was strange in that while the diggers were still cleaning out the tomb, they had found an inscription on the wall that described the story of Noah and the ark.

This raised two questions: why was the inscription there, and how did it get put on the wall of the king's tomb. This was Egypt, not the Middle East. What on earth would an inscription that bore a resemblance to the biblical Ark be doing on the wall of a king of Egypt? Egypt's religion was that of theism, a belief in one god, the god of the Nile River. There were many other gods the ancient Egyptians worshiped as well, like the Sun god, the Moon god, and the god of the harvest. The river was the lifeblood of this ancient marshland, and one need not offend the god of this river or else one's livelihood would suffer. The king also loved the occasional ride on his royal barge down this same river.

When the river flooded, it was thought that the Nile god was angry with her servants, and therefore, a penance must be made to appease her. On many occasions, the temple priests would perform the ceremony of Daku. In this ceremony, only those pure of heart would be offered as a sacrifice to the god of the Nile. The pure of heart was the firstborn son of the unlucky couple who happened to be picked from the lottery. This firstborn was wrapped in ceremonial clothing, and food such as sweet potatoes, corn, wheat, and barley lay around the infant. The priests would then offer a prayer to the Nile, and the baby would then be put into a sack with a weight tied to it. One of the priests would then go out onto the river with the struggling, crying infant while the other priests continued to pray, and when the priest got out to the middle of the river, the infant was then dropped into the river to drown, sacrificed to appease the god of the Nile and hopefully make the flood waters recede.

Dr. Mustafa met the professor at the airport in Cairo. After exchanging pleasantries, they got into the waiting car for the three-hour drive back to Mustafa's office and then on to the tomb. Time was of the essence, and they couldn't spend it getting Dr. James settled in, that would come later.

During the drive, they talked of times long past. Of digs that they both participated in and how the years just rolled on by. They reminisced of their old college professor Dr. Michael Dunkirk, who was a tenured professor at the university. He was an American-born professor who himself was a student of biblical archeology at the University of Tel Aviv in Israel. The professor graduated Magna Cum Laude and had himself participated in the excavation of the Red Sea area in which, according to the Bible, God had parted the sea in order to allow the children of Israel to cross over dry land.

Their old professor was very demanding not only of himself, but of everyone in his class. If he even thought one of his students was not applying himself to his studies, he would pick that student out of the class and tell him or her that a one thousand-word essay was expected of them as to whether or not that student actually believed that God would do such a thing.

No one wanted to be that student.

Dr. James, as luck would have it, did indeed become one of those students, as did his friend, Dr. Mustafa. It happened when they arrived back to the dorms late one night after spending the weekend blowing off steam. Their homework was almost done; just a few more hours of research to do, and then all would be well. But since they didn't realize that their term papers were due the following Monday, and not the next Monday, not only did they have to spend the week in the dorms finishing their term papers, they also had to write the one thousand-word essay on whether or not they believed God would part the Red Sea for his children.

Surprisingly, Dr. Dunkirk was impressed. This did not usually happen, not ever.

"So boys, I have to know. How did you do it? How on earth did you manage to write such an impressive essay on God parting the Red Sea?"

Ian spoke first. He was understandably nervous.

"Dr. Dunkirk, we had nothing but time, and nothing

to do but write the essay. That and we really hated being singled out as the ones to do this. I had to give up my date for the weekend, and Abu couldn't go home as he planned. Rather than sulk and get mad, we buckled down and just started writing. I'm going to have to do a lot of explaining to Amanda and buy flowers and chocolates for ditching her."

The professor couldn't help but to be impressed.

"Well, guys, I am impressed with your work. I hope this teaches you a lesson on why you need to have all assigned work in on time. You guys have a bright future in archeology. I know it's not the most exciting field to be in, but the travel is the most fun. It will take you to places you have only heard of or read about in books. Well, I have to go now, guys. I have some other people that need to know I expect an essay from them as well."

After shaking their hands, the professor said his goodbyes and walked away.

Ian James came from a Christian home. He was the son of a hellfire-and-brimstone Pentecostal preacher.

Needless to say, his father was animated behind the pulpit, and he wasn't afraid to let the congregation know it. Jonathan James felt the calling during his youth and had begun preaching right out of high school. Ian's father lived and breathed the Bible. After a few years of preaching, he enrolled in Liberty University to major in Pastoral Counseling. He was going to further his education of the Bible and continue to spread God's Word to all who would listen. It was in this same class that Jonathan met the woman who would become his wife, Pamela Jones. She was exceedingly beautiful and caught Jonathan's attention right off the bat.

He also caught her eye as well, but being the female she was, she just played as if she didn't know that he existed. She was majoring in Missionary Studies. She came from a family of Mormons but a voice inside of her was letting her know something was missing. They too were missionaries, but after several talks with her best friend, Melissa, who was a Christian, Pam began to question the teachings of the Church of Latter Day Saints and Joseph Smith. In that religion, even though Pam was brought up to believe that Jesus Christ is seen as the head of the church and that the church sees four books as authorities of the word of God; the Holy Bible, the Book of Mormon, Doctrine and Covenant and the Pearl of Great Price.[2]

Melissa took it upon herself as both a friend and a Christian to talk to Pam about this. After talking for a few days and Melissa showing Pam what the Bible says about other false doctrines, Pam gave her heart to Jesus. . After a much-heated debate and argument with her parents, it was decided that she should live with her aunt Betty, who herself was a Christian.

When she and Jonathan met, the sparks flew. They were married halfway through their senior year. They both graduated with honors, and he was about to go out into the world and preach the gospel to every creature. She went with him.

Ian was born five years into the marriage. He was their firstborn son, and they were going to teach him about the Bible, how God created the universe, and why a lowly carpenter named Jesus of Nazareth came to earth, was born of a virgin, grew up to become a preacher himself, was wrongly accused of blasphemy, and was condemned to die on the cross for mankind's sins.

When it was time to put Ian to bed, his father tucked him in while his mother read from the Bible. Ian remembered how much he loved this.

William was the second son of Jonathan and Pam. He and Ian were very close during their childhood. Will was ten years old when tragedy struck the James household. He was struck and killed by a drunk driver while riding his bike. The driver, who had a laundry list of drunken driving offenses, was put behind bars finally for twenty years after he was found guilty in court. This hit the teenage Ian hard, too hard. It made him question the wisdom of God. His parents tried in vain to teach him that although we don't understand God's wisdom or why he does the things he does, Ian would hear none of it. He ran away from home and moved in with his uncle David. David wasn't a follower of God, and Ian began to move away from his beliefs.

Ian graduated from high school and wanted to get away from home to see the world. Only he didn't have the money to do so. A friend of his parents, a certain Dr. Dunkirk who was also a classmate of his parents, offered to take the young man in and reacquaint him with the faith of his upbringing.

It was Dr. Dunkirk who put him to work in helping to write gospel tracts for the people in the local homeless shelter. In this way, Dr. Dunkirk could see putting Ian through college in the field of biblical archeology.

"Okay, Abu, so what's this about an inscription on the wall of the tomb of Ramses depicting Noah's ark?"

"All I can tell you is that it doesn't belong there. It makes no sense, none. We have scientists who are right now studying the inside of the tomb to see if there was anything else pertaining to the flood epic they may have missed. But I just can't understand why it's there or how it got there."

"Who found it?" Dr. James asked his friend.

"Someone with the museum who is fluent in ancient Egyptian Hieroglyphics, he was in the tomb with a pencil and paper making rubbings of the wall when he stumbled on that particular section," Dr. Mustafa replied.

"So how come it wasn't found when the tomb was being excavated? That tomb was thoroughly cleaned and catalogued soon after it was found, or so it seemed. The best archeologists around came to help with moving the artifacts out of there and making sure nothing was left for robbers to take. I don't understand how this could happen," Ian said to his friend.

"I tell you only what I was told and have seen. I myself wouldn't believe it until I saw it with my own eyes. I was still doubtful until I talked with the museum worker who himself found it. He told me that there is no doubt that this is indeed a reference to the biblical flood of Noah," Dr. Mustafa replied.

They were nearing the tomb. The driver let his passengers know that there was a crowd there, and not only that, but the media had somehow got word and were also gathered at the site. This was not good, not good at all.

"My word why is this happening? I specifically told Mr. Ahkmet not to divulge this information to anyone, especially the media. I knew that should they get hold of this kind of information we would have people show up here that have absolutely nothing to do with ancient Egyptian culture. I need to see Mr. Ahkmet at once," Dr. Mustafa said with loathing in his voice.

"Who's Mr. Ahkmet?" Ian curiously asked his now more-than-frustrated friend.

"He is the museum worker I was telling you about. I explicitly told him not to tell anyone about this, that we needed time to really look at the inscription to actually see what it says, what it talks about, to get to the actual meaning of it. It seems I can no longer trust him to keep a secret. Especially one with this much importance attached to it," Abu explained with a deep sense of disappointment about his associate.

Abu thought he could trust Tobruk Ahkmet. He considered himself fortunate to have him as a member of the museum staff. Ahkmet was not only well versed in ancient Egyptian culture and lifestyle; he could also "read the writings on the wall," so to speak. It is not an easy task to learn a new language, especially the language of the Middle Egyptians, which is a truly brutal language to master because it's a language not of words, but of pictures. Learning now to decipher what the words the ancient kings wanted to leave to their loved ones left there by the scribes was not an easy thing to do. This takes a long time to learn, but Tobruk was able to absorb what they had drawn on the walls and then in turn translated what was written.

Tobruk was a student of hieroglyphics at Bethlehem University in Israel. He was a very bookish kind of student, somewhat of a loner as well. He would much rather spend time in the university's library than talk to girls. Tobruk was the only child of a single-parent household. His mother died while giving birth to him. His father would read the Torah to him in the evenings after dinner, which served to spark his curiosity about the written word. One time he discovered a book about hieroglyphics at the school library, and he took it home to his father to ask him what the scribbles meant. His father told him what they were and that it took a lot of schooling to learn how to read them. Tobruk's father told him that was how the ancient Egyptians wrote their language. Tobruk decided that he would learn how to read this form of writing. He was going to become an expert in what these people said.

"Now not only do I have to show you that section of the wall so that you may see for yourself what I have been talking about, but I also have to find Mr. Ahkmet to ask him why he did this, why he would so such a thing. This puts not only the museum in a nefarious position, but also what's written on that wall," Abu said with measured constraint in his voice. He was ready to burst, but this was not the time to let his emotions get away from him. He had to remain calm and levelheaded if he were to find Tobruk and get some answers.

"Do you know where he is?" Ian asked with mild curiosity in his voice.

"He should be at the museum library. His job there is to translate hieroglyphics. Since he's the only one who can read them, he spends the afternoon doing just that. There are many writings he has to translate," Abu said flatly.

The driver parked the car. Ian and Abu got out and made their way toward the tomb. Ian couldn't help but to be both impressed and saddened at the same time. Impressed due to the number of reporters and onlookers at the tomb, and saddened for his good friend who was visibly angered at Tobruk for leaking this information. His trust in Tobruk had now been betrayed.

"Are you sure that Tobruk caused all this, Abu? Don't you think that someone else might have had a look inside the chamber and told someone else about it? On the way out here, you talked about him like he was a godsend to the museum because he was the only one who could read the pictures, and now you're thinking that he is to blame," Ian asked Abu.

Abu replied, "He was the only one who had access to the chamber except myself, he was also the last one who was in the chamber before I called you about this. It must have been him. Remember, he is the only one in the museum who can actually decipher those hieroglyphics. We put a guard on the door to the chamber; he had to show his access badge to the guard before entering. After this inscription was found, we took no chances whatsoever in guarding this find; it was of utmost importance that this be kept secret until we could actually take closer look to determine if what we were seeing was indeed what we were seeing."

A look of incredulity spread across Ian's face. It should not have come to much of a surprise to him as it did. He remembered how tightfisted Abu was with his money; he just didn't count on him being as tight with security as well.

Abu showed the guard his badge, he told the guard that Ian was with him, and they were both waved on through.

Although it was dark walking down the corridor, it wasn't so dark one couldn't see where he was going. This was because of the artificial lighting that had been put inside the corridor. Ian noticed how the walkway seemed to look as it would have three thousand millennia ago when the king was laid to rest in here. It was steep, and the way seemed to go on forever. They rounded a corner and walked for another few meters and came to a doorway. Abu gave the door a push, and they both walked inside the burial chamber.

Ian couldn't believe his eyes. The former burial chamber of Ramses the Great did not appear to him like the burial chamber of the pharaoh. The tomb was in a mostly destroyed condition. Even though Howard Carter first peered into it back in 1922 and in his words saw "the most wonderful things" it now looked like the proverbial hole in the ground. This former burial chamber of King Ramses (or KV 7, as it is now known, where the 'KV' stands for 'Kings Valley') had at the time of his burial been filled to its ceiling with the finest gold artifacts. The very throne on which the king sat would have also been laden with gold; but now, due to the many flooding events that have ravaged the tomb over the centuries has caused the moisture laden underlying shale to swell, giving the king's former tomb a very unkempt appearance. Besides the fact that tomb raiders stole the gold from the tomb years ago, it didn't look like the tomb of a former king.

Ian could only imagine what the splendor of this tomb might have looked like at the time of King Ramses burial. He had been in burial chambers before in his youth on archeological digs, and it had been a while since he had the opportunity to go on a dig again. He gave Abu a rather questionable look as he thought the museum would have made it a priority to make the former tomb look a little like it used to.

Abu was too busy looking at the very thing he brought Ian here to look at.

"See, this is the section of the wall that contains the flood account. It should not be here, because the ancient Egyptians did not believe in God. They worshipped the Nile as their god. Their very existence as farmers derived from the river," Abu pointed out to Ian.

"Well, if this is the case, then why would the king have allowed this kind of inscription to be carved into the wall of his chamber? Wouldn't something like this have been considered heresy because of religious preferences?" Ian asked.

Abu replied, "Yes, you are correct, Ian. But that is precisely the point, why and how did this get here? So far, no one can account for this. Virtually everyone who has studied Egyptian culture and lifestyle, such as me, knows that this should not be here, but yet, there it is. I am quite sure the pharaoh would have had the scribe who did this put to death for writings such as this. And now, due to Mr. Ahkmet's not being able to keep a secret, that too must be dealt with."

"So we first find out why he leaked this to the press, and then we find out how it got here. So it's a good thing then that this chamber has been catalogued," Ian replied.

"Indeed," Abu replied. "We have thoroughly catalogued this entire burial chamber. That and we also know who the scribe was who wrote this account of the biblical flood. We know everything about this chamber, except why that was written."

They exited the chamber and made their way back down the long, winding corridor back to the outside. The guard who was there when they walked in was not the same one as when they walked out. Abu looked at him curiously.

"Where is the guard who was here just a few minutes ago?" he asked.

"He left to go on a break," the new guard said.

"Do you know where he went to?" Abu asked him in a cautious tone.

"Well, since its end of shift, I assume he went home, sir," the guard answered back.

"Do you know what his name was?" Abu asked him

"No, sir, but he said he was new to the job, which is strange as the company isn't hiring right now. All of our positions are full," the guard answered back.

"So then if your company is not hiring, then do you know why he was here guarding the tomb?" Abu asked, his curiosity growing stronger.

"I couldn't tell you, sir. I don't do the hiring, but I do know that we are not accepting any more positions as guards. If you like, I can inquire of the management and let them know what went on here," the guard offered.

A curious look came over Abu's face. *Why would there be a guard here if there are no more of positions with this company?* Abu thought to himself.

"No, that won't be necessary. I will look into it. Thank you," Abu replied.

Ian said, "Sounds like trouble—a man guarding the tomb who isn't supposed to be there. What do you suppose this means, Abu?" he asked.

"I don't know, but I do know I don't like it, not one bit, Ian. But first things first, we must talk to Ahkmet," he said sounding none too happy with this entire ordeal.

CHAPTER 2

They walked into the museum; it was cool inside, which felt good. The summer sun outside was unbearably hot, and the air conditioning felt so good to them.

Ian let Abu lead the way. This was Abu's museum. He worked here, and he knew his way around. It had been a while since Ian had been inside a museum and took this opportunity to look around. Over there on display were some of the relic's of King Tutankhamen, the boy king of Egypt. Scholars were still studying his mummified body to see if there was any validity to the legend that the boy king was murdered. He died at the ripe old age of fourteen. No one knows why to this day.

The display showed how a chariot race might have looked if it were on a bigger scale. This was done in miniature, but it looked so authentic even now. Over towards the right corner of the room was a display that depicted what a market would have looked like in the pharaoh's day.

They made their way to the library where Ahkmet worked. As Abu ran his security card through the machine, Ian couldn't help but notice on what grand a scale this museum was built. He had been to so many museums, but this one looked as if it could have doubled as a cathedral.

The door opened slightly, and Abu gave it a push. The room was darkened somewhat so that the light wouldn't damage the relics being studied and poured over now. The room was immense. It gave one the impression that he could walk forever and ever in this room and not find his way to the other side. The room seemed to have an air of significance, an air of sophistication. Just standing there, it felt like the room had its own personality.

"This way Ian, Ahkmet works over there." Abu pointed out to his friend. He could see Ian looking around with extreme curiosity. Ian couldn't help but to be absorbed into the ambience of this room. He seemed to forget why he was there.

As they approached Mr. Ahkmet, he was absorbed into his translations.

"Mr. Ahkmet, I need to talk to you," Abu said with an air of urgency in his voice.

"Oh, hello Dr. Mustafa, so good to see you again. I am making such good progress with—" Abu cut him off.

"Mr. Ahkmet, why did you leak to the media the information on the wall of the king's chamber! You knew this was supposed to be kept a secret!" Abu tried as hard as he could to keep his voice down, but it was difficult.

"Tell the media? Me tell the media? I can assure you, Dr. Mustafa, I did no such thing." Ahkmet replied to the extremely mad Abu.

Mr. Ahkmet leaned in to tell Abu assuredly, "Why on earth would I do such a thing? Mr. Mustafa, I can assure you that I fully understand, just as you do, the importance of this find. I can also assure you that I fully understand the reasons why this must be kept a secret from even the most prying eyes."

Abu just stood there, looking at him, not believing a word he was saying. The look in his eyes told Tobruk that he was treading on dangerous ground. But he really had no idea why.

"Ahkmet, you are the only one who has access to the chamber. You are the only one who knows how to decipher what's written on that wall. You are the last one who was in there before this mess happened. Now, tell me, Ahkmet, why should I not fire you right here on the spot?" Abu was furious indeed.

Ian just looked on with his hand on his chin, observing Mr. Ahkmet. Watching how he talked, how he answered Abu's questions, his body language in general. Ian observed how, with every question Tobruk was asked, he fired back an answer without so much as batting an eyelash. He didn't seemed one bit perturbed by this third degree Abu was giving him. To Ian, Tobruk was telling Abu the truth.

"That is not true, Dr. Mustafa. You also have access to the chamber. But it is also true that I alone know how to translate the hieroglyphics, sir, but I can assure you with the utmost truthfulness that I had nothing to do with the media being here." Tobruk was doing everything in his power to convince Abu that he was telling the truth. That he had no idea how the secret of the king burial chamber came to light.

Tobruk Ahkmet continued, "Mr. Mustafa, the guards are there twenty-four hours a day guarding the entrance to the tomb. No one can gain access without wearing the same badge that you and I are wearing. The guards can't even go in as they don't have the same level of security that we do," he explained as matter-of-factly as he could.

"Wait, speaking of the guards, the guard who was there when we entered the tomb was not the same as the one there when we left. He said it was shift change, but I was in such a hurry to let Ian here see the wall that I didn't give it a thought." Abu realized he had not introduced his friend.

"I'm sorry, Mr. Ahkmet. This is an old friend of mine from college. I called him here so that he could see for himself the writings on the wall. Tobruk Ahkmet, may I introduce Mr. Ian James, professor of Egyptology at the University of Oregon in the United States. He is here to see if he can lend validity to our find," he said.

"Pleasure, Mr. Ahkmet. I've heard a lot about you from Dr. Mustafa here. He tells me you're the one working on translating the hieroglyphics found within the tomb relating to the flood epic. How far have you gotten?" Ian asked in a pleasant tone.

Tobruk answered, "I have all but finished. I think I can say that most people are familiar with the story of Noah's ark in one way or the other. The ancient Mesopotamians themselves told the story of Noah in the epic of Gilgamesh."

"Ian, we must inquire about this guard that was there at the tomb when we entered. According to the other guard, he wasn't supposed to be there. There has to be a reason for this, and I don't like the feeling I have about it. Something is wrong, terribly wrong," Abu said very glumly. He couldn't help but notice the sinking feeling in the pit of his stomach.

Abu went to the phone to dial the number to the security agency that was hired to supply guards for the tomb. The secretary answered.

"Good afternoon. Nile Guard Agency. Rina speaking. May I help you?" *Rather pleasant voice,* Abu thought to himself.

"Yes, good afternoon. My name is Abu Mustafa; I am head of the Nile River Museum. I am inquiring about a guard you have working here guarding one of our tombs. I need some information on him please."

"It's our policy not to give out any personal information, sir, but if you could possibly tell me the nature of the information you need, I might be of assistance to you," she said into the phone.

"I don't know his name, but I was told that he was a new hire. He was working at the tomb this afternoon. I would just like to know when he was hired by your company," Abu asked her in just as nice a tone as he could muster.

He could feel his frustration growing again.

"A new hire sir? I don't believe we have any new hires, but if you give me a few minutes, I will access the company roster to see if we have hired anyone recently," she told him.

Abu waited for what seemed like an eternity. Ian was

busy looking around at the relics being studied; Tobruk went on with his translations.

Her voice came back to his ear. "No, sir, I'm sorry. We don't have any new hires recently. We haven't hired anyone in the past few months," she offered.

"Are you sure? Can you look again please? The guard working today said the guy was new, maybe he hasn't shown up on your roster yet," Abu replied. *Surely, there must be some mistake. After all, this is a security agency; wouldn't they know who was working for them and who wasn't?*

"One moment sir, I will look again," She said, beginning to get frustrated herself. She knew she wasn't stupid, but she sure didn't appreciate calls like this. She put him on hold again.

"Incredible, why does it take so long to find anything about someone who works for you? Why can't she find out any faster?" Abu was now reeking with frustration. Ahkmet was now looking up from his work; Ian was still looking at relics.

Again, she came back in his ear. "Sir, I'm sorry, but we show no new hires either recently or in the past few months. I'm looking at the most current roster we have. It's updated to just last week," she told him, trying hard not to let him know what she was thinking; she was tired of his call.

"Thank you very much," Abu said as he hung up the phone.

Darn, was it possible that someone did get access to the tomb that wasn't supposed to? And if so, then who could it have been?

Ian chimed in, "Abu, maybe we should go back to the tomb; there might be an answer to the question of the supposed newly hired guard."

"Tobruk, how close are you to finishing with the translation?" Abu asked.

"Another hour should do it, Dr. Mustafa," he answered.

"Mr. James and I are going back to the tomb to look the outside over. Hopefully we have an answer to this mess by that time. Stay here and continue doing what you're doing please," Abu told him with an air of urgency to his voice. He wanted nothing more now than to find the person who let the media in on this.

CHAPTER 3

Outside the tomb, Ian and Abu began to look for anything that didn't belong. They looked for a security guards badge, a hat, something that would give them a clue to this stranger who was guarding the tomb but they could find nothing. It seems this unknown guard had done his homework and after a few minutes of looking they headed back to the museum. On the way back, Ian stopped to buy a sandwich from a vendor who was selling them to the workers at the tomb. He was eating it while walking with Abu. Just before they reached the door, Ian put the wrapper in the trashcan, but as he did, something at the bottom of the can caught his attention.

He looked inside the trashcan. Although it was covered with a small amount of trash, what caught his attention looked rather interesting. He bent down to get a closer look. Abu looked at him curiously.

"See something interesting, my friend?" he asked.
"Abu, it looks to me like we found a clue to our new friend." he replied.

"What do you mean?" he asked in a cautious tone of voice.

Ian reached inside the trashcan and pulled out a

complete guard uniform. On it was the insignia of the Nile Security Agency.

They looked at each other in complete surprise. They had found the one who had told the media the information about the writings on the wall. But now there were many questions about this mystery: who was he, and why was he so interested in the writings on the wall of the tomb? They also wondered if this strange guard knew how to interpret the hieroglyphics; if so, why they would be this important to him. According to Mr. Akmet, he was not the one who informed the media of this information. If it was not him, then could it have been the stranger?

Chapter 4

He pulled out his cell phone and dialed the number. "The package has been delivered, Mr. Swanson." He looked around as he talked; making sure no one was listening.

"Well done, Mr. Mahmood. I trust you encoded it before you e-mailed it to my computer?" Mr. Swanson asked, wanting to make sure that such a message would not fall into the wrong hands. He had plans for this package, and no one was going to stop him.

"Of course sir. We both know the sensitivity of these photographs. You should have it in your e-mail now," Mahmood replied.

"Good. My man will put your payment where you have directed. You will find the amount a little more than previously agreed upon, a little something extra for your hard work. I will keep your number in case I need you for another mission," Mr. Swanson told him.

Montgomery James Swanson III, the distinguished senator from the great state of Utah was born into money on July 4, 1943, and graduated from Joseph Smith High School in 1960. Monty's great-grandfather had founded Swanson Insurance Group in 1912; two years after a man named Henry Ford created the first Model-T's. Business was slow at first because people were still used to the horse-and-buggy mode of transportation that was still prevalent at that time. But over the years, Monty's great-grandfather, Richard James Swanson, along with two of his banking friends who were investors was determined to keep the business afloat. After their first decade in business, they already had assets in the millions of dollars. Now, with all the company's assets combined, they were worth billions.

During his high school years, he was elected class president twice, president of the debate club twice, ran for president of student council twice but was defeated by his next-door neighbor James Monroe Quigley II both times, but he came back the last year of school and won. Monty was also captain of his football and basketball teams respectively. His high school résumé was most impressive. He also was elected class valedictorian. Monty always did have a way with words.

After graduation, he was accepted to Harvard University, with a double major in political science and government. He excelled in his classes and was making friends with his charismatic personality. Monty graduated Magna Cum Laude.

Now, it was on to Yale to study biblical archeology. The young Mr. Swanson had aspirations to study the Bible and to see if all those events in the Bible really happened. It was during this time that he met his best friend for life, James Madison Thurgood II. Monty found it interesting that James shared his name with one of the past presidents of the United States. James was taking his major in political science at Yale; they both knew they wanted to be United States senators.

It was at Yale that James had introduced Monty to his group of friends who were members of an organization that stood for the civil rights of others who couldn't speak for themselves. The group was immediately impressed with the young Montgomery James Swanson III and accepted him into their organization. Monty felt good about these people and their cause, although they weren't too comfortable about his desire to confirm biblical events. To them, the Bible was just a book, and they took every opportunity to tell him so. Eventually they got through to Monty, who decided that he wanted to be a member of this organization more than he wanted to prove the Bible. The name of this organization was the American Civil Liberties Union.

CHAPTER 5

The American Civil Liberties Union was founded in 1920 by Roger Nash Baldwin, Crystal Eastman, Albert DeSilver, and others. Roger Nash Baldwin was born in Wellesley, Massachusetts, on January 21, 1884. When he graduated from Harvard in 1905, he taught sociology at Washington University in St. Louis from 1906 to 1909. Baldwin was a pacifist, and when World War I broke out, he joined Abraham Muste, Norman Thomas, Scott Nearing, and Oswald Garrison Villard to form the Fellowship of Reconciliation.

Abraham Muste, born in Zierkzee, Holland, on January 8, 1885, and his family moved to the United States in 1891. His roots were of the conservative background, his father being a supporter of the Republican Party and a minister in the Dutch Reformed Church.

Muste became increasingly radical in his views and in 1912, he supported presidential socialist party candidate Eugene Debbs. On the outbreak of World War I, he left the Dutch Reformed Church and became a pacifist. In 1919, he moved to Boston, where he found work with the American Civil Liberties Union. In the early 1920s, Muste worked as director for Brookwood Labor College in

Katonah, New York. There, he also joined the Fellowship of Reconciliation and in 1940 was appointed executive secretary of the organization. In this position, he led the campaign against the United States involvement in World War II. As executive secretary of the Fellowship of Reconciliation, he gave permission for James Farmer and Bayard Rustin, both pacifists, to establish the Congress of Racial Equality. After the war, Muste joined with David Dellinger and Dorothy Day. Dellinger was a radical pacifist; Day was a socialist and pacifist. Together, they founded *Direct Action Magazine* in 1945. Dellinger upset the political establishment when he criticized the use of atomic bombs on Hiroshima and Nagasaki. In 1953, Muste established the War Resisters League and helped influence civil rights leaders such as Martin Luther King and Whitney Young to oppose the Vietnam War. Muste died on February 11, 1967.

Crystal Eastman was born on June 25, 1881. Her parents, Samuel and Annis, were church ministers. She graduated from Vassar College in 1903, and obtained a degree in sociology at Columbia University in 1904 and at New York University Law School in 1907. Eastman settled in Greenwich Village and joined a community of feminists there. In 1907, Paul U. Kellog, who was editor of the social work magazine *Charities and the Commons,* hired her to investigate labor conditions for the Russell Sage Foundation's Pittsburgh Survey. During the year, she conducted the first-ever in-depth sociological investigation of industrial accidents ever undertaken. In June 1909, Charles Hughes, the governor of New York, appointed Eastman to become the first woman member of the Employers Liability Commission. She married Wallace Bendedict in 1911, but the marriage ended in divorce. Her reputation as a political campaigner grew in 1913, and later that year became a delegate to the Seventh Congress of the International Women's Suffrage Alliance in Budapest, Hungary. During the conference, she met Aletta Jacobs (pacifist), Emmeline Pethick-Lawrence (feminist), and Rosika Schwimmer (socialist.)

As a pacifist herself, Eastman was a strong opponent of World War I. Soon after the outbreak of the war, she joined with other pacifists to establish the American Union against Militarism. Over the next couple of years, the organization lobbied against America's possible involvement in the war. It also lobbied against the draft and the arms trade. In 1916, Crystal married British poet and fellow anti-war activist Walter Fuller. In that same year, she turned over AUAM duties to her friend Roger Baldwin. The following year, she helped establish the National Civil Liberties Bureau. She worked with her brother and fellow radical, Max Eastman, on the journal *The Masses,* until it was shut down by the government for its opposition to America's involvement in World War I.

They then joined with other radicals, such as Art Young and Floyd Dell, to establish the socialist magazine *The Liberator.* In 1922, *The Liberator* was taken over by Robert Minor, who was himself a member of the communist party. Crystal Eastman then began writing for *The Nation.* While she and her husband were blacklisted for their left-wing political opinions, they moved to London. While in England, she worked for both *The*

Daily Herald and *Time and Tide,* which were feminist journals. Her husband, Walter Fuller, died of a stroke in September of 1927. Upon his death, she returned to the States but was herself in poor health and died of a brain hemorrhage on July 8, 1928.

Norman Thomas was the son of a Presbyterian minister and was born in Marion, Ohio, on November 20, 1884. He studied political science under future president Woodrow Wilson at Princeton University and graduated in 1905. Thomas did voluntary social work in New York before studying theology at the Union Theological Seminary. He was influenced by the Christian Socialist movement in Britain and became a committed socialist. He was ordained in 1911 and became pastor of East Harlem Presbyterian Church in New York City. As a pacifist, he believed along with his associates such as Crystal Eastman and Roger Baldwin that World War I was an immoral, senseless struggle among rival imperialisms. Thomas joined with fellow pacifists and socialists to establish the National Civil Liberties Bureau, which in 1918 became the American Civil Liberties Union.[3]

CHAPTER 6

Monty checked his e-mail. Sure enough, the package was there, complete with pictures of the writings on the wall of the tomb of Ramses. This was worth the extra he gave to Mahmood for his work. The pictures were sharp and precise and showed in graphic detail the inscriptions of the flood epic.

He turned on his television.

"Back to our main story: a subject of truly epic proportions written on the wall of Ramses the Great who was king of Egypt during the great plagues that are mentioned in the Old Testament book of Exodus in the Bible. For more on this story, we take you to John Maxwell with the latest. John." The news was all abuzz.

"Tim, the story here at the tomb of Ramses the Great is one of absolute incredibility. Found on the wall of the tomb was an inscription of the flood that supposedly took place during the time of Noah. The reason this story is so important is that this story is written on the wall of the tomb of one of the greatest kings of Egypt. Ancient Egypt didn't believe in any one god, but they worshipped many, such as the god of the Nile River, the sun god, and the moon god, to name but a few. It is believed that Ramses was the king during the time of the great plagues that were inflicted upon Egypt; furthermore, some religions say that Moses was visiting the king on behalf of the God he worshipped.

"For a story such as this to be found here is quite extraordinary. This hasn't as of yet been verified by the museum, but we are waiting for that to happen, and that should come at any time now. Back to you at the studio, Tim."

"John Maxwell reporting live from the tomb of Ramses," Tim Davidson, KRPT news anchorman said as the cameras turned back to him.

"This has become better than even I imagined," Monty said to himself. In all his wildest dreams, he could never have imagined the media would have jumped on this story like they did, but then again, look at the storyline and look at where it was found. So of course the media would jump right on it. Good dogs.

Monty called his old friend James Thurgood to tell him the good news.

"Jim, Monty here. I have the package on my computer, and I'm looking at it right now. It looks real good, partner, and it's surprising to look at actually. The whole story is here. My man took several pictures of the wall and the inscription. Most of the pictures are close-ups, and you can see how good the definition is. When you see this, you will be just as impressed as I am."

"Good. Very good. What are your plans for this information, Monty? Where do we go from here?" Jim asked in a curious, albeit cautious, tone of voice. He knew the kind of impact this information would have on religion, but when the actual authentication of these pictures came out, someone needed to be there with a rebuttal of the authentication.

Jim wanted it to be Monty, but from the tone of Monty's voice, it sounded like Monty had other ideas.

"Well, ol' buddy, for starters, who said we have to do anything at this point in time? Do me a favor, my friend, and let me do the worrying about this thing, okay? You are the one who makes the plans for the rebuttal of authentication, and let me be the one who takes care of this information, okay?"

Monty knew his associate was the nervous type, and they had been friends for over for over forty years, but sometimes, even he grew tired of Jim's hysterical personality. Monty remembered forty-one years ago when Jim was helping him to develop the case in which Madelyn Murray O'Hair was attempting to sue NASA for the astronauts reading the first chapter of Genesis from the space capsule in the late sixties. They lost that case and Jim has held that against himself ever since.[4]

"Okay, Monty, okay. You know how I get sometimes. But this is *big*, and we can't afford to have someone else get their hands on it. I will lay low on this, but you be very careful about how you handle this. Agreed?"

"Yes, Jim agreed. Now, how are you going to rebut this information when it comes out? Have you thought that far out yet?"

"No. Not yet. But I know I am a better speaker than you, even though you do have a silver tongue. But I will know what to do when the time comes."

"Agreed. So then, I will talk to you later about this. Don't worry, Jim; everything will be okay."

Monty hung up his phone and continued to look at the pictures his contact had sent him. Even he couldn't believe the clarity of the pictures of the wall here on his computer. As he scanned the pictures, he couldn't help but notice the newness of the inscription. After all this time, over three thousand years after being scratched into the wall of the pharaoh's tomb, and being in the darkness for that amount of time, there was hardly any type or kind of wear on that portion of the wall.

It almost looked as if the story had been carved there yesterday. *But that yesterday was over three thousand years ago,* Monty thought silently to himself.

He opened a drawer to his desk, took out a writeable CD, put it in the computer's tower, and with a few clicks of the computer mouse, he downloaded the pictures onto the CD. After a few more seconds, the CD was finished. Monty took it out and wrote "Pictures" on it. He opened the drawer again and put it back where he got it.

It was late, and he was tired. Monty got up from his desk. He was happy with himself that the plan was going so smoothly thus far. His man in Egypt had been able to disguise himself as a tomb guard, gain access to the wall inside the tomb, take at least one hundred pictures, walk out unnoticed, get to a computer, and e-mail him those same pictures. Life was good. Now all Monty had to do was safeguard the disc from anyone who didn't need to see those pictures. Since he locked his office up at night, there would be no one who could get to the disc. He walked over to the chair on the other side of the office and put his suit coat on. He went to his office door, opened it at the same time he turned off the light, and closed the door behind him.

I have to share this with my ACLU associates tomorrow. They, too, will be just as pleased as I am, Monty thought to himself as he walked down the hall to the elevator. He pushed the down button and heard the elevator begin to make its ascent. The door opened; he got on and pushed the button to the first floor. He loosened up his tie and unbuttoned the top button, relaxing a little.

The elevator door opened, and Monty walked out and went to his car.

What a day, he thought to himself.

CHAPTER 7

Tobruk continued his investigation of the inscription. So far, he couldn't see any reason not to give his blessing to its authentication.

It's remarkable, and it's fantastic. I have not seen anything like it, but so far, it looks authentic to me, he thought to himself.

"Abu, even if Tobruk gives this thing his blessing, will you believe it's real?" Ian asked his friend, wondering if Abu could actually bring himself to believe that something like this of a biblical nature could be found on the wall of an Egyptian pharaoh's tomb.

"Ian, my personal beliefs withstanding, I would believe Tobruk if he gave it his blessing. Why on earth would something such as this be on an Egyptian pharaoh's tomb? The more I think about this, it produces more questions than answers. There is no logical reason it should even be there, but yet, there it is. I'm quite sure Moses didn't have anything to do with it, as he was too busy getting the Israelites ready for the trip out of there. One thing is for sure here, Ian: the inscription is there.

"But how it got there is anyone's guess. I think we should concentrate on the here and now, and not worry about the details. We could actually spend a lifetime wondering how all this took place, and how it got there. I can only hope that it is real," Abu said with a serious tone in his voice.

At that time, Tobruk walked through the door.

Ian and Abu turned toward Tobruk with a wondrous look in their eyes. Dead silence followed.

"Well?" was the only word spoken by Abu.

"It is as it says! It is the story of Noah and the ark!" Tobruk said with excitement in his voice.

"Tobruk, are you *sure? Are you absolutely sure that this thing is authentic?*" Abu asked of his friend.

"Yes, I give you my word that this is real," Tobruk spoke with sincere passion in his voice.

"Well then, we need to immediately contact the world's most learned biblical authorities on this matter, get a second opinion. We need to treat this with the utmost care. Tobruk, you keep the door to the library closed and sealed off. I will make the appropriate contacts and get them here. The media will also want to hear of this, but I'm not too good at speaking to them," Abu said with a bitter taste to his voice.

"Abu let me handle the media. As many digs as I have been on, I have learned how not to speak to them," Ian said, grinning as he spoke.

"Very good, my friend," Abu said, sounding both relieved and pleased that Ian would also help.

Tobruk walked to the library and closed the door behind him. He walked over to the section of the wall that was taken out of the tomb and brought here, and he gazed down at it one more time.

In his own mind he found it hard to believe that this could possibly be real, and yet, here it was. He ran his hands over the hard surface, feeling the grooves of the symbols that had been carved here three thousand years before.

Incredible, that I would see something such as this in my lifetime, Tobruk thought to himself. Tobruk decided he needed some pictures of this inscription. He made a mental note to bring a camera from home after all the excitement wore off and take some pictures of his own.

I must call the senator and inform him of this. He will be most pleased to hear that in my opinion, this inscription is real.

Tobruk walked over to the library phone, picked up the receiver, and dialed the senator's number.

CHAPTER 8

Senator Carlton Monroe Chraft, or Carl to his friends and family. The distinguished senator from the State of Utah and past high school classmate of Senator Swanson had a rather impressive resume.

After graduating from Joseph Smith High School, he had applied to several colleges; most turned him down due to his grades not being sufficient enough for any Ivy League colleges. He was class president of the student council and co-captain of both the football and basketball teams. He had to work harder than his classmate Monty to get the grades needed for an Ivy League-type of education. He was smart and he knew it, but the scores on his SATs didn't exactly reflect his ambitions. His father owned his own business, and his mother was working at a time when working mothers were frowned upon for not being the typical stay-at-home mom. His father, William, owned William Chraft Freight, the largest trucking firm in the entire state. His grandfather, Robert, had started the business from the ground up. He had been a truck driver during WWII and after his discharge he decided to go into his own business. He borrowed money from the local bank and bought his first eighteen-wheeler, making long-haul trips all over the state and country. Carl remembered the stories as a kid his father used to tell him about the heartburn his grandmother used to go through when Grandpa went out on trips delivering freight and materials to customers locally at first, but within the year, he was also driving to places all over the state. After the first five years, Robert had earned enough money to buy a small fleet of five trucks, and also employ the same amount of drivers to man the trucks; one of those drivers, was his own father. He remembered how his grandmother would tell of the tremendously long hours away from home her husband had to spend in order to not only earn money to support his family, but also to buy more trucks.

Robert wanted to own a fleet of trucks and be the best long-haul business in the entire state. During his summer vacations from high school, his father would put him to work both driving trucks locally and also loading the trucks for other drivers who were headed out of state, within the state, or to the local area.

In the space of ten years, Robert had a fleet of twenty trucks and was the premiere long-haul service of not only the county but the city and state as well.

Robert also began to participate in the local county school board. They began to teach Darwin's theory of evolution, and Dad didn't like that kind of stuff. Sometimes, he would take his son, William, with him to these meetings, where he would watch his father talk, reason, and negotiate with the other members of the school board who disagreed with his father on this subject. He watched as his father would give his opinion on evolution, the Bible, and how the two just didn't mix. Carl became fascinated with how his father worked the board members. He noticed how his father never seemed to lose his composure or his temper. His father negotiated with the other members of the board, trying to get them to come to his own conclusion that evolution was a subject best left to theory, and not to any high school textbooks. Ultimately, however, the other members of the school board didn't agree with his father and voted to allow evolution to be taught in high schools in the county.

It was also at that same time, that his father decided that it should also be fair to let the biblical version of creation be taught alongside evolution. However, a middle-aged atheist from California, Madeleine Murray O'Hare, came out on national television and opined her opinion as to why creation, the Bible, or simple prayer should all be outlawed in any public arena, especially schools.

Carl got his interest in politics from his father and, in his junior and senior years of high school, ran for president of the student council, and twice beat a kid named Montgomery James Swanson, who was running for the same position.

In his senior year of Joseph Smith High School, he applied for Harvard, Yale, and Columbia. All of them turned him down. Then the rumor around school was that Monty Swanson was accepted to Yale for the start of the fall semester. It was not a rumor, however.

He then applied to and was accepted to Brigham Young University to major in government and politics. He wanted to go to an Ivy League college, but his mother and father were both happy that he would be going to college in the state. He would be going to college only a few hours away. Besides, Brigham Young might not be an Ivy League school, but it still was not something to be ignored. A lot of very bright young minds came out of that institution, and now, Carl was going to be one of them.

While in college, he excelled in his studies, attaining an honorable mention on the college's dean's list. He also met a young man by the name of Doug Ketcham. Doug was a very bright, cheery sort of fellow. Carl liked him from the beginning.

Carl also noticed that everywhere Doug went; he was carrying a small black book, which he thought might have been the Book of Mormon. This was a Mormon-run school after all. Carl decided he would ask his buddy about why he was carrying the Book of Mormon around with him everywhere he went. Doug told him there was another book that made more sense, was easier to read, and didn't have all the contradictions the Book of Mormon had. Doug told him he was carrying around the Holy Bible with him. Intrigued, Carl asked him about it. During the next few hours, they both shared with each other their personal faiths and how each of them was raised. He was raised in the Mormon religion; Doug was too, but he was also introduced to the Bible by a friend of his that had moved into his neighborhood before the start of his senior year of school. This friend told him about Jesus and how he was born of a virgin, grew up, and was crucified for mankind's sins. Doug told him that at first he didn't believe in what the Bible had to say, but his friend was determined to tell Doug about his faith. Doug was invited to church one Sunday morning, and heard the sermon. Doug answered the altar call that morning and had been carrying around the Bible ever since. Before they went to eat dinner that evening, Carl got on his knees with Doug and accepted a new kind of understanding, a new kind of faith. After that, he couldn't get enough of the Bible and what it had to say. He had a particular interest in the story of Noah's ark.

He had kept that same interest all through his college years and also throughout his political career as well. Carl became one of the distinguished gentlemen from the state of Utah.

Carl had also followed the writings of a certain biblical archeologist and grew even more fascinated by not only his findings but how he wrote of them as well. He kept up with this archeologist, who also had tenure at the University of Oregon. His name was Dr. Ian James.

CHAPTER 9

"Senator Quigley, Tobruk here. I have authenticated the inscription; it is indeed the epic of Noah. We will have other authorities here within the week to give their authentication as well. I will take pictures of it and send them to you as quickly as possible. Do you have any other orders?"

"No, Tobruk, keep doing what you're doing, but get me those pictures as soon as you can. And also safeguard the section of wall with the story on it. *It must be preserved at all cost.* Do you understand?"

"Yes, I understand. I will take and send you the pictures soon."

"Very good Tobruk. Keep me posted."

With that, Tobruk hung up the phone and walked back over to the inscription.

He went to the door of the library, opened it, and closed the door behind him. He went back to Abu's office.

"Sir, have you contacted the people you need to come here and see the inscription yet?"

"Yes Tobruk. They will be here at the end of the week."

The sheer number of people that showed up for this was nothing short of amazing. The number of media that also showed up was enough to dumbfound the most media-savvy person. There were reporters from CNN, ABC, NBC, FOX, CBS, and other media outlets. That was not taking into consideration the number of newspaper reporters who were there as well. Most of the on-air media were simply reporting from outside the museum, as access to the tomb had not yet been granted. The air was buzzing with excitement.

"Ian, the experts are on their way. I am wondering how we are going to keep control of this situation with all the press that is here now as we all know that the last thing we want is a group of reporters who will somehow get this all wrong." Abu said with a bit of sarcasm in his voice.

Both of them got into the museum van and were on their way to the airport. They pulled up to the front gate of the airport and got out. They went inside to the terminal and welcomed the experts of several different religions to Egypt. They welcomed Rabbi Josef Macholic of the Israeli Jewish Temple. After him was Dr. Mohammed Nadir, professor of Biblical Studies at the University of Egypt at Cairo; Dr. Jim Brannigan, chancellor of Bible Baptist University in Orlando, Florida; and finally, Cardinal Dumas Frencheti, dean of Biblical Studies at the Catholic University in Rome, with an emphasis on the Old Testament.

All men were welcomed cordially, and then it was back in the van and back to the museum.

The Luxor Museum is located in the old city of Thebes. Here, one can find displays such as pottery, jewelry, furniture, and statues. One can also find displays of ancient Egyptian culture and kings.

The boy king, Tutankhamun's relics are on display here. The real attractions also on display here are those of Tuthmosis III, dating from 1436 b.c. This is on the first floor. The two hundred and eighty-three sandstone blocks that form the wall from the ninth pylon of the Karnak Temple are here as well. There are also carefully selected items from the Theban temples and necropoles. One of the many good things about the Luxor Museum is its proximity the Valley of the Kings.

The history of the Valley of the Kings is quite impressive. The Greek writer, geographer and historian Strabo, who lived in the first century BC and Diodorus Siculus, the Greek historian whose forty book prose that is referred to as the Historical Library and who lived in the first century AD reported that the total numbers of Theban royal tombs was forty-seven, which at the time only seventeen were believed to be undestroyed. The Greek traveler and geographer Pausanias, who lived in the second century AD is famous for his Description of Greece, which is a lengthy work that describes ancient Greece from firsthand observations. He, among other ancient writers remarked on the pipe like corridors of the valley, referring to the tombs.

Some of these travelers left their names and other marks. The earliest datable graffiti in the Valley was found in the tomb of Ramses VII, and can be dated to 278

BC, and the latest was left by a governor of Upper Egypt was dated to 537 AD. The French scholar Jules Baillet counted over two thousand Greek and Latin graffiti left over the classical centuries, along with a lesser number of Phoenician, Cypriot, Lycian, Coptic, and other languages. Almost half of these were found in the tomb of Ramses VI, who was considered to be the fabled Memnon himself. After the Arabs came into Egypt in 641, interest in the Valley waned considerably. It was not until the end of the sixteenth century that once again travelers began to take notice. One of the first travelers to record what he saw at Thebes was Frederic Louis Norden, who was a Danish adventurer and artist.

Father Claude Sicard, who was head of the Jesuit Mission in Cairo, traveling in Egypt between 1714 and 1726, who visited the Valley in 1708 and located ten open tombs including that of Rameses IV. He wrote of the extensive wall paintings and their colors. Father Sicard's notes for the most part were unfortunately lost, and thus the first significant published account of the valley was left to an Englishman named Richard Pococke in 1743. He apparently noted signs of about eighteen tombs, though believing that only nine of these could be entered.

When the first cache of royal mummies was discovered 138 years later in 1881 at Hatshepsut's temple of Deir el Bahri, world attention was once and for all focused on the quiet valley, and the first of many new excavations began in the area. Victor Loret had been appointed as the Director-General of the Antiquities Service, established by August Marriete in 1856.

Only five days after he began to dig below the cliffs under the Qurn, or "Horn" mountain, his team discovered the tomb of Thutmose III. He added sixteen mummies to the map of the principle valley. He also discovered the second cache of royal mummies within the tomb of Amenhotep II.

Loret was not very well liked; when he left, his post was open. Howard Carter was then appointed as antiquities inspector for Upper Egypt. His responsibilities were to maintain all the sites of Upper Egypt and to grant concessions for others to dig, rather than having the authority to dig on his own. One of Carter's claims to fame in this job was that he installed the first electric lighting, handrails, staircases, and running boards in the royal tombs. Carter had this job for six weeks in 1903. He resigned and never worked for the Antiquities Service again. In 1922, Howard Carter found the last and possibly the most well known of these tombs, that belonging to the young King Tutankhamun. It lies directly opposite the tomb of Rameses IX. For all the amount of treasure that had been found in this tomb, the space itself is small and all but one room was undecorated.

Directly across from Tutankhmun's tomb like KV5, where work continues to uncover what may be the last resting place of the one hundred and fifty sons of Rameses II. Since Carter's find in 1922, many more tombs have been found, and many more have been ravaged by tomb raiders and thieves. Rameses VI had one of the largest tombs in the valley. His tomb is decorated with scenes from the books of the underworld, and the burial chamber is dominated by the shattered remains of the king's massive granite sarcophagus.[5]

Chapter 10

They pulled up to the front of the museum. The religious scholars could not believe their eyes. Before them were multitudes of media reporters of all outlets. The museum apparently had to post a guard at the entrance in their absence. It was a long drive to and from the Cairo airport. Once inside, Abu led them to the museum library and the section of wall the inscription was found on. The workmen had removed the part of the wall the inscription was found on and had taken it to the museum for further study. Rabbi Setcham Macholic got out his copy of the Torah and began to pray in the tradition of the Jewish rites. Dr. Brannigan and Dr. Nadir began to study the inscription, and Cardinal Frencheti began to look it over as well.

Between them, they had over seventy-five years of biblical scholarship to fall upon for just such an occasion.

After Rabbi Macholic finished praying, he too began to study the wall. Even though the rabbi had been brought up in the traditions of his ancestors, he had also seen too many copies of biblical relics in the marketplaces of his hometown. In seeing this inscription, he couldn't help but to be skeptical of this as well. He remembered that he also had once seen a relic of the chalice Jesus used at the Last Supper that a vendor was selling. Once the amazed tourist bought it, the vendor simply waited a few minutes and put another one that looked just like the last one out on the shelf. Setcham Macholic promised himself he wouldn't be fooled like that in his lifetime.

"So, gentlemen, this is the inscription I was telling you about. Please take your time and look everything you see over. You'll see that it has nothing to do with the Epic of Gilgamesh. However, study it and we think you'll find that it does indeed fit the biblical description of the flood and of Noah's Ark. Yes, it did come from the pharaoh's tomb. The 'how's and whys' of why it was found in the tomb has no purpose here. It was found, and your job now is to come together and authenticate its existence. Can we agree on this?" Abu said as he stepped back and let the scholars go to work. There could be *no* doubt in any of their minds about this inscription.

"Yes, we all agree on what we need to do while we are here, Dr. Mustafa. I must say, however, I find it incredulous that this was found inside the tomb of an Egyptian pharaoh," Rabbi Macholic admitted. Knowing what he knew, all logic seemed to be suspended for him at this point in time.

"I assure you, Rabbi, its real." Abu pointed out to him. "I must also ask how long will it take for you to authenticate this find?" Abu asked.

"It might take a few days, it might take a week. We will also need to go to the tomb itself and see if there was anything that was missed that might also be related to this. I'm sure that in all the excitement, something very well may have been missed," Jim Brannigan said to Abu.

"Indeed. I will take you there myself. Just let me know when you wish to go there."

All the scholars collectively nodded their heads in agreement that they would let Abu know when this needed to happen.

In the meantime, Ian was outside the museum dealing with the media.

"First of all, I'd like to thank everyone for coming. I know this was on such short notice, but I can assure you that we now have a team of religious experts working on this inscription. Not only are they working on it, but they are also studying the hieroglyphics to determine the validity of the inscription. I can also tell you that this team of experts has informed me that they are quite confident that it is real but that further study is needed."

Brandon Smith of FOX news asked the first question. "Dr. James, when were these religious scholars brought in to look at this inscription, and how much experience do each of these people have?"

"Between them, they have almost seventy-five years of experience. If they can't figure this thing out, no one can."

"Dr. James, John Maxwell, KRPT news. Is confidence high on whether or not these scholars will all agree that this is real? If not, what happens if they can't agree?"

"Good question; however, that is out of my knowledge and experience. I can only tell you what I know about them and what they are in the process of doing. I ask that you please be patient, and I will keep you informed as to events that unfold during this time period."

Ian thanked them for their time and turned to go back inside the museum. He silently praised himself for not giving out too much information. But then again, there wasn't really all that much information to give out in the first place.

He went inside the library and gave Abu a nod to let him know the media had been dealt with.

"How's it going?" he asked in a hushed tone.

"It's going fine. They are still looking at it, studying it, and comparing it to the biblical version. Tobruk is translating for them."

"Any idea how long this is going to take?"

"Not at this time. They have said it might take a few days or a week. Things like this do take time, especially due to the location of the find."

Ian let out a long sigh. He silently hoped this wouldn't take that long.

The scholars looked at their subject all week, looking this up, looking that up, all to verify this inscription. They knew what they needed to do, but yet they just couldn't logically give in to this thing being of biblical origin. The rabbi alone was fighting an inner battle with himself as to whether or not this thing was actually real. The others were also doing the same thing with themselves. There was no logical reason that this should even be considered to be of a biblical nature, yet there it was right in front of them.

Jim Brannigan, Cardinal Frencheti, and Dr. Nadir all

looked upon this inscription in sheer disbelief. To them, this shook each of their faiths down to its core, not that they *didn't* believe in the Bible, since it is God's Holy Word after all, but for the inscription to have been found inside the tomb of an Egyptian pharaoh was really making them reach. It gave new meaning to the phrase "God works in mysterious ways."

At the end of the week, the scholars had a closed-door meeting with each other in Abu's office. They all agreed that the proper tests had been done on the inscription and all the proper research had been completed. *Was there a stone left unturned? Did they do all the right things?* In all actuality, each agreed that what could be done had been done. The only thing left to the imagination was the *why* and *how* of such a thing being found in a pharaoh's tomb. They also all agreed, was just something for time to solve, if it ever could be. After the meeting, they had another one with Ian, Abu, and Tobruk.

"We have spent a considerable amount of time on this, as you all know. We have done our tests, studied it, dissected it, and prayed about it and over it. We have done everything we can and know how to do.

"In the end, gentlemen, we can come to no other conclusion that this seemingly biblical inscription of the epic of Noah's flood and of the ark, even though the location of its finding to us is nothing short of incredulous, is, as we all agree, authentic and real." Dr. Brannigan spoke for all the scholars, who in turn nodded in approval of Jim's speech.

Could it be possible? Is it real? They had all come to an

agreement; they were all in complete compliance about this. The museum had such an extraordinary find on its hands. Something of such magnitude came about only once in a lifetime.

Abu and the rest sat completely spellbound.

He was the first one to speak. "You all agree together that this is the real thing, and it is indeed authenticated? Of this there can be no doubt in each of your minds. You know what you were brought here to do, and you know the result of that collective decision? So, I ask you all again, do you all agree that this is real and of biblical origin?"

Abu wanted to clarify this absolutely. He knew that once they released word of this to the world, every nut case and press member would have a field day. The last thing he wanted to do was to give the museum the proverbial black eye over something so unique. This would mean astronomical amounts of income for the museum, as well as tourism dollars and all the free publicity in the form of the media.

Abu felt sort of bad thinking in terms of dollars and funding, but they only had one chance to get this right, and he had to think about the museum. For him, the strangeness of finding a biblical passage about Noah's Ark in an Egyptian pharaoh's tomb was a bit hard to wrap his head around. That is also why he felt they needed to get all of this right the first time, the last thing he wanted to wind up being was another religious statistic, another so-called religious nut who wanted the Bible to be believed so bad he would be made to look like they thought the whole thing up. Moreover, most everyone knew the God of the Bible was not the one worshipped in this land. The ancient Egyptians had many gods.

That and each of their personal reputations was also at stake.

"Dr. Mustafa, again, I speak for the group. We all agree that this is of biblical origin, and it is indeed real. We can't clarify why it was found inside an Egyptian tomb, but you didn't bring us here to find that answer. This is the real thing; of that, we are all sure."

Even though it shook them to their cores, Jim spoke with confidence and reassured Abu and the rest of their conclusion.

"Well then, Ian, can you handle the press again? And Tobruk, can you figure out where this thing will be put on display within the museum? I will need to begin to figure out how to handle publicity for the museum."

Ian and Tobruk each nodded in the affirmative and accepted the responsibility that Abu gave them. Abu asked the scholarly gentlemen if they could each give a statement to the press about how they came to the conclusion they did. Each agreed to do so.

Ian checked his watch; it was five in the afternoon. The press had been waiting patiently all that week, during which a few interviews had been granted. Each member of the press had asked the same questions, albeit in a different manner. They got the same answers. He would announce a press conference for nine the next morning.

Cardinal Frencheti asked Abu the same question that was on all the scholars' minds.

"Dr. Mustafa, although we have collectively agreed

that this inscription is authentic, still, this does not explain how or why it got on the wall of the pharaoh. Is, or has there been, any clue as to the whys and how's of all this?

"Someone must know. Have any records been found of who that particular scribe to the pharaoh was? Whether this pharaoh's personal beliefs were not what he was presenting to his subjects? This again raises more questions than answers. I must admit that I personally am flabbergasted at what I have seen here this week, as are Drs. Brannigan and Nadir and Rabbi Macholic. We have been talking amongst ourselves this entire week about the origin of this inscription. We have also been wondering if there is any way to dig deeper into this pharaoh's past. Can we find a way to discover who the royal scribe was?"

This man had a lot on his mind, as did his associates. This was completely understandable, seeing it from their point of view. *How many times have I thought the same thing about this epic on the wall? It makes no sense, absolutely none, yet, there it is,* Abu thought.

"Well, I suppose that is possible. We have been so consumed with this finding recently that I don't think anyone has really asked that particular question."

Tobruk took this question.

"I can tell you that to the pharaohs, scribes were just that, scribes. The pharaohs didn't really bother themselves with the particulars of 'which scribe will I use today' type of thing. When the pharaoh wanted something to be recorded, he called for a scribe and one would be there ink and parchment in hand."

"It is true that scribes were used to document

everything about the day-to-day lives of pharaohs. But they were also used to document which decision he made that day, who he had executed, who owed him any type of payment.

"The scribes documented an unbelievable amount of information from day-to-day tasks. Most importantly, however, the scribes were used to document the very life of the pharaoh. How he came to power, whose son he was, his standing in the house of the previous pharaoh. Look at the wall of any pharaoh's tomb out there, and you will see the result of and the documentation of everything that pharaoh did both during his life and his reign. To actually look up a certain scribe for a particular king just wasn't considered to be important. Scribes were basically hired help."

Tobruk explained this to the small gathering. Each face showed the look of both understanding and slight disheartenment. If any question could or should be answered, it's this one.

Ian got up and started for the door.

"Where are you going, my friend?" Abu asked.

"I am going out to face the press and let them know that at nine tomorrow morning, we will have a conference and all or most questions will be answered and that our esteemed colleagues here will also try and answer all their questions. Hopefully, it won't get too ugly," he said matter-of-factly.

"Indeed. Well, gentlemen, I will call this meeting adjourned for the day, and thank you for your most kind help with this issue. I will walk with you out to the van and drive you back to the hotel. Tomorrow will be a rather busy day."

Abu got up, shook hands with the scholars, and waved a hand to indicate that they should leave. As they walked past the many displays, Cardinal Frencheti couldn't help but notice the display to King Tutankhamen. *King Tut was a very rich pharaoh indeed,* the cardinal thought to himself. The sheer majesty of this display to the boy king seemed overwhelming, to say the least.

Jim, Nadir, and Setcham were all equally subdued by the displays before them. They were so consumed by the finding in the king's tomb; they had not noticed the displays on site.

Cardinal Frencheti was amazed at the boy king's monumental display. Over in the far left corner of the room, Jim Brannigan, Setcham Macholic, and Nadir were all looking at the Cleopatra display.

The amount of gold adorning this display was incredible.

Soon, they began to feel the day barge in on them, and so it was time to climb into the van and head back to the hotel, shower, eat, and call it a day. Tomorrow would come early, and each had to prepare something for the media, and the public watching them.

They climbed into the van, and Abu got into the driver's seat and began the fifteen-minute drive back to the hotel.

As they said their goodbyes to each other, Tobruk went to the hotel lobby, got out his cell phone, and made a phone call.

CHAPTER 11

"Senator, Hasan speaking. The ark inscription has been authenticated by the scholars. We are now at the hotel with them. There will be a press conference tomorrow morning at nine. Each scholar will give their insights into why they believe the inscription is real. We will then take them back to airport in Cairo and see them off."

Hasan was quick and to the point with the senator. He knew the senator didn't want a lot of details about this. All the senator would want to know is if the inscription had been authenticated. It was and by a very respectful panel of religious experts from different ethnic backgrounds. There was no way anyone could claim this was a fake. After the press conference, events would be set into motion by the ACLU to investigate these same scholars, and he knew this. If there were any way this organization that attacks anyone's opinion that doesn't agree with them could be legally dissolved he would be the first one in line to do it. As it was, they were legal and there was nothing anyone could do about it.

The senator got on the phone to his associates in Ankara and told them what the tentative plans might be if all went well. He then called Hasan back to tell him what he must now do.

The press conference started right on time. Abu looked a little nervous but excited at the same time. He didn't want anyone asking the same stupid questions, like they did the first time, about how the inscription got there in the first place. *We are long past wondering about that,* he thought to himself. He wanted to get this over with as soon as possible.

Ian stood next to him and saw the sea of people who were just dying to ask questions.

They all looked as if it was feeding time at the local trough. There seemed to be reporters jockeying for position closer to the podium, but this was not a large room, and neither they, nor the scholars had anywhere else to go. Tobruk scanned the room for anyone *too* eager to get information.

"Ladies and gentlemen, thank you for your patience throughout this whole week. I know many of you have questions, so let's start with whoever has the first question."

It seemed Cardinal Frencheti was also eager to get this over with.

"Cardinal Frencheti, what makes you think this thing is real, and how do you think it wound up in a pharaoh's tomb?"

So much for wondering about that, Abu thought to himself again.

"This inscription is indeed real. My fellow scholars and I have spent the past week doing test after test and comparing it to other flood epics in other languages and cultures. As for how it got there, who knows? For those of you still wondering the same thing, you might try asking any experts in Egyptology that same question. Now, please, can we have questions that deal directly with the inscription itself?"

The cardinal settled that subject once and for all.

"Cardinal Frencheti, in comparing the inscription to other flood epics and cultures, what is the one thing that stands out in your mind that makes this the real thing?"

That is a good question, all of them thought.

"The one thing that stands out in my mind is that it tells the story *exactly* as it is written in other languages and cultures. We have spent considerable time in this, and to me that alone is what authenticated it."

Rabbi Macholic stepped up to the microphone.

"I have never seen anything like this before, but I can assure you that I, too, agree with the learned cardinal. I have been a student of the Bible, the Talmud, and have also studied the Dead Sea Scrolls intently. To me, this is nothing short of a miracle. Elohim be praised." The Messianic rabbi from Chicago said, raising his hands.

"I think in all our minds, we still don't understand how

this got to where it is, but I also know that in the back of our minds, we can't help but to wonder. At the same time I think it's most important to realize that, just as the rabbi said, this can be truly considered to be nothing short of a miracle. Maybe it's not for us to know the answer to that question, but to just be thankful it was found, and found just as intact as the day it was carved on the wall. Thank you all for your questions." Dr. Brannigan stepped in and settled it once and for all for the rest of them. Each of them gave him an approving glance.

The last question was for Abu.

"Dr. Mustafa, now that the inscription has been authenticated, what will happen to it? Will it be put in a room? Will it be on display? Can you tell us where the final resting for this will be?"

"It will be put behind glass on display, with a plaque in front of it proclaiming its authenticity. Tours will still be held during regular hours," he said matter-of-factly.

The press conference was over, and it was time to take these scholars back to the airport. As the van pulled out, Ian couldn't help but be amused.

"What's so funny, Ian?" Abu asked.

"Just the look on all their faces when Dr. Brannigan stood up there and basically answered *the* question that everyone still had in the back of their minds, and how he put it to bed rather quickly. You would think that the last thing on all their minds was answering questions at a press conference."

All of them had amused looks on their faces.

"Oy, I didn't want to be answering stupid questions all

morning long. These people are *meshugana;* they are crazy. I wasn't too sure about it until the third day of staring at it that it was real. How many times can reporters ask the same questions in a different way and get the same answer?" Rabbi Macholic said sounding glad the whole ordeal was over.

"What I don't understand is that they all looked as if *we* were *lying* to them. As I was talking, I saw more sideways glances than at any other time during this talk. I know it's not a logical thing for something of this magnitude to be doing inside a pharaoh's tomb, but we weren't the ones who put it there," Dr. Brannigan said, saying what the rest of them were silently thinking.

Soon, most of them were fast asleep, with the exception of Abu who was driving. It was a long drive to Cairo.

On the long drive back to Thebes, Tobruk sat in silence, contemplating his next move. He knew what he must do, and that was to have Ian and Abu pack their belongings as soon as possible when they got back. The senator would want to meet with them as soon as they landed. Of course, this was expecting a lot from his associates. Tobruk would have to find a way to convince them to pack and to get on a plane to meet with a United States senator. He would just have to explain it the best way he knew how.

"Why so silent, Tobruk?" Abu asked.

"It's a good thing the scholars all agreed that it was real; you should be just as excited as we are," Abu added.

"I am just thinking about what went on earlier," Tobruk said.

"Well, I wouldn't think too much, Tobruk. We've got

a bottle of champagne waiting for us back at the museum. There is much publicity and revenue coming Abu's way for the museum," Ian told his friend.

Hasan sat back and watched the scenery go by. He thought to himself, *why couldn't the airport have been built closer by?* The drive from Cairo to Thebes was long indeed, at least a four-hour drive, and he so hated long trips. Now, the thing to do when they got back was to have a talk with his friends about what they must do next. Now that the inscription got the blessings of the scholars and now that they were on their way back to the States, Hasan also knew that they too must be on their way soon. The question was how he could convince Ian and Abu that what they must do now was of the most urgent importance.

Ian turned to look back at Tobruk from his passenger side seat; something was eating at his friend's mind, of that he was sure. He never saw Tobruk sit and think like this before. The only time Tobruk did this was when he was translating the inscription, and this he did with utmost excitement. Now, he was sitting in the backseat looking forlorn and solemn. Not at all like him. The sun was setting on the Nile.

Chapter 12

It was a long drive back to the city of Thebes. Ian was sitting silently in his seat, watching the evening traffic go by. Abu was on his cell phone talking to the museum and instructing them to double the guards around the inscription. Tobruk was still amazed at the find inside Ramses the Great's tomb, and he knew it was real the first time he read it. But it was a good thing to have had these religious scholars and experts look at the inscription, study it, and validate it themselves. Of course, during the past week, having the press from all over the world spread the word didn't hurt. Abu did not like having them there, but he was using them as much as they were using him. The press used him and the find as the story; he used them to get the word out. Tobruk knew he must phone the senator and tell him the news. Tobruk knew the senator would be both excited and cautious.

Excited at the authenticity of the find and cautious in how to handle the next step in finding the ark, Tobruk also knew that he must call the senator when he was alone as he knew that if he were to tell his friends what must be done next, they might not be too cooperative. He sat in silence, watching the Egyptian sunset and beginning to feel more relaxed. Abu hung up his cell phone and looked at Tobruk, who looked lost in his thoughts.

Ian turned the radio on, and a song they were all familiar with began to play. He and Abu began to sing along. Tobruk smiled and shook his head. It was late that evening when they got back to Thebes. They stopped at the museum so that Abu could ensure that there were two guards posted on the inscription and that running guards would be making their normal rounds inside the museum. The museum's head of security spent the next thirty minutes assuring and reassuring Abu that everything and everyone was in place. The head of security, who was a friend of Abu's family, understood the gravity of this archeological find and the importance of it. Once Abu was assured that all precautions were in place, he and Ian and Tobruk left for the night.

They went to Abu's house. Abu was single but had a two-bedroom apartment overlooking the Nile. Abu prepared dinner for himself and his friends. He made a meal of lamb and chicken shish kabob with pita bread and dipping sauce. They took the meal out on Abu's balcony, which afforded a very well lit night time view of the Nile. They ate heartily as it had been a long day in talking to the media, getting the scholars to the airport and coming back to the museum to ensure that security had been elevated around the inscription and coming home. After dinner, tea was served and conversations of the day's events began. They talked of the excitement surrounding the finding of the inscription in the pharaoh's tomb. They laughingly speculated on any number of theories on how it found its spot on the wall of pharaoh's tomb. They talked of how the press asked the same question in all different sorts of ways and how Rabbi Maholic, in his own blunt and honest way, let all of them know that it is indeed real, and how the other scholars did very well in keeping a straight face as he said this. As the conversation wound down, Tobruk began to tell his friends about a matter of utmost importance.

"Ian, Abu, I must tell you both something very important," Tobruk said with a very serious look in his eyes. Ian and Abu both looked at each other first as if to silently ask each other, *what's wrong with him?* Tobruk immediately had his friends' attention. Ian spoke first.

"Tobruk?" he asked in a somewhat surprised tone of voice.

"What's on your mind, my friend?" Abu finally asked.

"About the inscription," he began. "We are all happy it has been authenticated by those who are smarter than I about such things. But now, there is another matter of utmost importance I must face, but I would also appreciate your help. The man you see before you is not who you know; I am not the man I have been pretending to be."

Ian and Abu again exchanged glances. *What does he mean he is not the man we think he is?* They both asked each other silently.

He continued, "My real name is Dr. Hasan Habib, and I work for a distinguished United States senator who has been fascinated by the ark since he was a boy. He made it possible for me to be around the ark inscription as soon as it was found. I have been talking to him all week while the scholars were busy themselves in authenticating it. The senator has asked that I enlist both of you to come with me to Ararat to find and document the ark, and he is prepared to pay you both handsomely for it. Ian, he is prepared to deposit five million dollars into your account should you agree to go along. Abu, for you he is prepared to bestow a large endowment to the museum and also to you personally for your help as well."

Ian and Abu both sat back in their chairs in stunned silence. It was one thing for this man who was formerly known to them as Tobruk to now reveal himself as Dr. Hasan Habib, but to also go on a rant about some senator who was willing to pony up both a rather "handsome" sum of money and a large endowment to the museum with something extra for Abu.

"Tobruk," Abu said, "What are you talking about?"

Dr. Habib continued. "I'm sorry, my friends, but I have had to keep my identity a secret until the inscription could be verified. There are others who would like to ensure the ark is never found," he said, noticing the skeptical look Ian and Abu's faces. He couldn't blame them; if he weren't personally involved in this, he wouldn't believe himself. A police siren began to wail as he got up from this chair and turned to face the balcony. He walked over to the railing and rested his hands on it. Hasan stared down at the traffic going by. It was Friday night, and the traffic was heavy as usual. Traditional Egyptian Muslims were at home observing the Sabbath; the rest of them were enjoying the weekend.

"So, who are you really? First, you said you were Tobruk, now you're saying you're Dr. Hasan Habib. Who are you going to be next, Ramses the Great or Seti the first?" Ian asked angrily.

Abu sat with his arms folded across his chest and had one eyebrow risen as if to demand that he answer Ian's question.

I must calm them down and make them believe, he thought to himself.

He turned to face his associates, took a deep breath, and began to tell his story. "My friends, again, I am sorry to present my true self in this way to you, but again, I work for a United States senator who is very interested in finding and documenting the ark. He has had a fascination with it as I have already told you, since he was a child. I apologize once again for the secrecy, but I remind you there are others who don't want the ark to ever be found. I had to keep quiet until the scholars were one hundred percent sure of what we had found. When they gave us the thumbs up, I immediately called the senator to inform him. But also, another phone call was made to another senator—one who does not want the ark to be discovered. He will stop at nothing to ensure that this does not happen. The senator that I work for is Carlton Monroe Chraft."

Ian and Abu silently pondered Hasan's words, and then the questions began. Ian asked the first question.

"Why is this Senator Swanson so interested in the ark, and why is he willing to pay so much money to have someone and find it?"

"Not someone—both of you," Hasan answered. "The senator wants the ark found no matter what the cost. If he has to drain the family fortune, he will do so," Hasan finished, sounding so matter-of-fact.

Abu asked, "So, who is this other senator that doesn't want the ark to be found, and why is it so important to him that it not be found?" Both were very good questions, and Hasan was going to answer them with as much detail as he could muster. The senator wanted and needed their help, and it was his job to persuade them to do so. The senator had told Hasan that if he needed to, to call him as a last resort to prove that Hasan was not lying. Carlton Monroe Chraft wanted to talk to Ian and Abu face to face and not over the phone.

"How much money did you say Senator Chraft wants to pay me to find the ark? Not only that, but given the political climate of that region, does he think that the Turkish government will just let us climb up that mountain and start taking pictures? Politically, that whole region is not stable to say the least, and if anyone goes there, it will take months of planning and putting a team together to carry supplies, not to mention a guide. Has the senator thought that far ahead?" Ian asked, wanting to know how connected and powerful the senator was, as a politician, to the Turkish government that he could pay both him and Abu to climb the mountain given that the political climate was not very friendly.

Hasan noted that from the way Ian was speaking, he had made up his mind. "Does that mean you have decided to go, Ian?" He asked, cleverly hiding his anticipation.

"It does sound intriguing, I must admit. But who is this other senator that doesn't want the ark to be found?"

"Five million dollars to answer your first question."

"I didn't think senators made that kind of money."

"His family fortune is worth many, many times that."

"Well, how much is he really worth?"

"Do you want more money, Ian?"

"I'm just curious. Five million dollars is a lot of money."

"Ian, Mr. Chraft's family is worth billions."

"Hasan, who exactly is Carlton Chraft?"

The look on Abu's told Ian he was taking the words right out of his mouth. "Mr. Chraft is one of the heirs to the Chraft Trucking fortune. I'm sure that as both a professor and Egyptologist you've seen their trucks unloading some of your findings from your digs at the university you work for."

"As a matter of fact I have. Their company is under exclusive contract to transport any and all archeological findings in all digs associated with the university. I guess I just never put two and two together." He realized that Senator Chraft could indeed afford five million dollars. *An heir to the Chraft family fortune, the senator only needs the job as a hobby,* Ian thought to himself.

"To answer your second question," Hasan said, interrupting Ian's thoughts, "the senator has anticipated your willingness to go. He has a team waiting for us in Ankara as we speak."

"Let's talk about the endowment for the museum,"

Abu said, very much interested in what Hasan had to say about that.

"Abu, the senator believes a check in the same amount as Dr. James for the museum should suffice, unless of course you disagree, and in that case, he is willing to negotiate your terms for coming with us as well. That is assuming Dr. James has agreed to go on this expedition."

Ian told Hasan, "I want to hear this from the senator's own mouth. The money does sound good; Hasan, but I can't cash the promise of an associate of a politician."

"Understood," Hasan agreed.

"The things I could do for the museum with that kind of money—" Abu said aloud.

"The senator would be most happy to discuss this matter with you, Abu," Hasan informed his friend. "So do I call the senator and tell him to have three plane tickets for us at the counter first thing in the morning?" He asked with his thumb already on the call button with the senator's number dialed in on his cell phone.

"Call him," Abu said. "Let's see how serious this guy is."

Ian nodded his approval. Hasan punched the call button, and in his ear dial tones began their chorus. A few seconds later, he heard a male voice on the other end.

"Senator Chraft," the voice said.

"Senator, this is Hasan. I have the most wonderful news. Dr. James and Dr. Moustafa have both agreed to meet with you tomorrow afternoon. Can you have tickets waiting for us first thing in the morning at the counter? Splendid, see you tomorrow afternoon, sir."

Hasan hung up his cell and told Ian and Abu they must begin packing at once.

Chapter 13

Ian and Abu hardly slept. Ian kept thinking about the money the senator was offering him and just how much influence Chraft must have with the Turkish government that would make them agree to allowing not just an expedition, but an American one at that, go up that mountain. At this point in time, the American government was not particularly welcome anywhere in that part of the region. During the build-up to the Iraq war, the Turkish government turned down the United States' offer of thirty-seven billion dollars to use that nation as a gateway into Iraq. So again, just how much influence did this Chraft guy have with the Turkish guys? As he was packing some clothes, a shaving kit, some snacks, a CD-player with CDs, and some towels, the alarm on his wristwatch began to chime. It went off as the preset hour of six o'clock marched past. Ian had actually been up since five in the morning talking to himself and shooting the occasional glance toward the window as the morning light became brighter.

He was definitely intrigued by the five million-dollar offer but also by the thought of actually being able to go up that mountain. Maybe the senator really did have that kind of influence, being a politician, but that was the senator's business. Right now, however, the senator just needed to show him the money.

Abu had also been up pacing the floor in his room. The museum was his life, and he loved Egypt and its ancient history. He remembered reading a book on the pharaohs as a high school student and was hooked on the history of his native land on the spot. He did appreciate to some extent the Western culture that began to make its presence known in the early seventies, but Abu made up his mind that he would become an expert in the history of Egypt and join the faculty of a museum. He went to university where he met Ian, and now he was the curator of the Egyptian Antiquities Museum. He had met those goals in his life. The museum, however, could always use the endowment. Museums were always in need of finances for maintenance, grounds keeping, displays, paying the employees, or electricity—take your pick. In Abu's mind, finding the inscription was a good enough run of luck, but to now learn of this United States senator who wanted to give a rather large endowment to the museum was an offer that he had to explore. Would the Turkish government let them in? He did not know and was not a politician, but this Chraft guy seemed to be resourceful enough to not only give the museum an endowment but get them to Ararat. If Chraft could do that, then who was Abu to argue? Besides, if the ark was up there and they were able to document and take pictures of it, not only would that make a good display, but it would also generate more income.

This was a win-win situation. Hasan was watching television and having coffee in the living room when Abu and Ian came out of their rooms. He poured each of them a cup and put the cups on the dining room table. Abu spoke first. "Thanks, Hasan. I needed this. I hardly slept last night. I'm bushed."

"Same here, but we can sleep on the plane," Hasan answered him back.

"Speaking of which, what time does our plane leave, Hasan?"

"Our flight leaves at noon. We must be on our way very soon. I have already called the terminal and our tickets are waiting. We will have a twelve-hour flight," Hasan said as he drained the last sip of coffee from his cup. He was noticeably agitated as they began to make their way to the front door of Abu's apartment.

"You okay, Hasan?" Abu asked with a smug look on his face.

"I am fine, my friend. I am just anxious to get in the air."

The taxi was waiting as Ian opened the door and they walked outside. The driver got out of the car to help load the luggage in the trunk. After everyone was situated in the car, Hasan spoke to the driver in Arabic of their destination. The driver nodded, checked his side and rearview mirrors, and proceeded down the alleyway toward the main street. The driver turned the radio on, and traditional Egyptian music filled the car. Hasan and Abu began to sway and sing to themselves. The song had a rapid beat to it, but both of them and the driver, whose name was Sadin, were singing the same words along with the song. Ian sighed deeply and put his headphones on. He pushed the play button, and Def Leppard's song "Pour Some Sugar on Me" filled his ears. While Ian began to sing to himself, Hasan, Abu, and Sadin all gave Ian a mild look of boredom and slightly shook their heads—*Americans.* By the time they arrived at the airport, they only had forty-five minutes to check in, get the tickets, and board the plane. Sadin parked the car, and they all got out getting their luggage. Hasan paid Sadin, who wished them well and got back in his cab and began to drive off. A passenger flagged him down, and he pulled over to pick up the next fare. Hasan was even more agitated now that they could not get on the plane fast enough, and it was showing in the way he was acting.

"My friends, we must hurry. There is no time to waste!"

He began to break into a flat-out run with Abu and Ian trailing behind him. As they got to the United flight counter, he asked for three tickets under his name. Hasan, Abu, and Ian were in the system. The clerk asked to see their passports, and after comparing pictures and expiration dates to faces, tickets were printed out and given to them. Bags were checked, and then it was again off to the races as Hasan sped toward terminal C, gate F, with Ian and Abu once again in tow. The plane had already begun to board as they arrived at the gate. They walked up to the clerk who took their tickets, put them in the machine, and spat them out the other end. She gave their tickets back to them, and it was hurried walk down the ramp. They got to their assigned seats—Hasan had an aisle seat across from Ian who also had an aisle seat, and Abu was seated right next to him. He was much calmer now. After instructions from the flight crew on emergency procedures, the plane was hooked up to a car that pushed it away from the terminal.

Once the plane was safely away from the terminal, the car unhooked, and the plane began to rev the engines and taxi toward the runway. The captain's voice came over the intercom, and he thanked the passengers for choosing United and told them food and drinks would be served when they were at cruising altitude. The plane made a sharp right-hand turn and stopped. The captain asked the tower for permission to take off. Permission was granted, and Ian, Abu, and Hasan felt themselves being sucked back into their seats as the captain pushed the throttle forward putting the engines to one hundred-percent power. As the plane got down to almost the end of the runway, the nose lifted skyward, and the rest of the plane followed. The co-pilot flipped a switch, brought the wheels up, and they were on their way to America.

CHAPTER 14

At the cruising altitude of thirty-five thousand feet, the pilot flipped a switch, and the seatbelt sign went dim. People began to rise from their seats to use the lavatory and retrieve items from the overhead bin. The flight attendants began preparing the in-flight meals. Hasan got up from his seat and knelt down beside Ian. He began to talk as Abu leaned toward him from his window seat.

"My friends, I must thank you for coming. Senator Chraft will be most pleased."

Abu asked the question that was on his and Ian's minds. "Hasan, who are you really? And how did you get involved in all of this?"

It was a good question, and now was the perfect time to answer.

"My birth name is Hasan Habib. I am the oldest of five children born to Halil and Satipo Habib, who emigrated from Egypt to the United States in 1965. My mother gave birth to me shortly after their arrival. They settled in Salem, Oregon. My father was educated, and he accepted a teaching position at the university there. My father taught ancient Egyptian history, and when he would come home at night, he would teach me everything about my culture and heritage. We spoke our native Egyptian tongue only at home and spoke English outside the home. I grew up learning about the pharaohs, their culture, religion, gods, everything. I became fascinated with that time period. After high school, I went to the university to study Demotic, or Late Egyptian language. It began to be written in New Kingdom around the Armarna period. Armarna is a city on the east bank of the Nile River in the modern province of Minya and is also one hundred ninety miles south of the Egyptian capital of Cairo. After graduation, I moved to Washington D.C. to begin work at the Smithsonian Institute and began cataloguing and interpreting the thousands of volumes of ancient Egyptian writings they had, along with further documenting paperwork describing the discovery of the tomb of the boy-king Tutankhamen. Even though Howard Carter discovered the tomb in 1922, there was still much work to be done as for the first time the museum was going to host the King Tutankhamen exhibition and I was helping to get things ready. I was out in the main hall instructing the workers on where to put the artifacts that were coming in. After this was done, I began work on the hieroglyphs that also came in. It was during this time that a man named Clayton Chraft, who was a friend of the museum curator, arranged to come in and look at what would become one of the museum's finest exhibitions.

"I was in the back room reading one of Howard Carter's descriptions of his search for the boy-king's tomb. The curator, Mr. Thompson, introduced Mr. Chraft and I. After the introductions, Mr. Thompson asked if it would be okay if Clayton stayed a little while to watch my work and ask questions, as he, too, was a history buff. I told him I would be delighted to talk to him about my work. We wound up talking for hours. We talked of our families, how we grew up, and how our personal beliefs formed. After this, he began to tell me of his fascination with Noah's ark and how it had been his life's ambition to go up the mountain to find the ark. But now, he was getting on in years but would love to find someone with the youth and the will to go up the mountain and find it. The time came for him to leave and for me to start closing things down for the evening. He gave me his business card as we said our goodbyes and shook hands. Before he left, he told me he was putting together a team to go Turin, Italy, to document the alleged burial cloth of Jesus Christ, and he would love for me to be a part of that team. A few weeks later, I called him to let him know I had some free time coming and would love to go on this trip he had put together. Then, with ticket in hand, we were flown to Turin, but something had gone terribly wrong. As soon as we arrived, the people who were supposed to pick us up from the airport were not there. Someone else had shown up instead. They acted friendly at first, but when we left the airport going in the opposite direction of Turin, one of the team reminded our driver of our destination. The man in the passenger seat turned around and put a gun in his face. This man told my associate—"

"Excuse me, sir; what would you like to eat? We have roast beef, and we have chicken," the flight attendant said as she interrupted Hasan's account of how he met the senator from Utah.

"We will talk about this later," he said as he turned to retake his seat. Ian and Abu each had the roast beef; Hasan chose the chicken. All three men were famished as they began to eat. As they continued to eat, Ian and Abu began to discuss discreetly the possibility that everything Hasan had told them was a lie. Abu mentioned that if it were not true, however, then why were they on a plane to Washington to meet with this senator?

"Let's see what happens," Abu told him.

After they finished the in-flight meal, all three men began to settle back into their seats and relax. Ian had closed his eyes and was beginning to drift off to sleep, while Abu was looking out the window. After watching a few clouds pass by, Abu's eyes also began to get heavy. He closed the blind to his window, put his pillow next to his head, turned out his light, and began to drift off to sleep. In a few minutes, the flight attendants came back to collect their trays. After the trays had been collected, all three men settled back in their seats for a nice long twelve-hour nap.

CHAPTER 15

"Excuse me, sir, you'll have to put your seatback in the upright position and fasten your seatbelts. We're thirty minutes away from landing. Thank you," the flight attendant said to a still-groggy Hasan. Coffee would be such a good thing right now, he thought to himself.

"Ma'am, what time is it right now?"

"It's seven o'clock; we will be landing at seven thirty," she replied. Hasan looked over at his friends who were themselves beginning to wake up. Abu looked out over the Washington D.C. skyline, which was all lit up and bustling with activity. Ian was also looking over Abu's shoulder to get a better view. They both saw the Washington Monument, all ablaze in the light of its own towering glory with the reflecting pool in front of it. Directly opposite of this monument to America's first president and commander in chief stood the Lincoln Memorial, built to honor that president who freed the slaves with a stroke of a pen; his statue looked larger than life. The memorial was bathed in light along with the rest of the city. Behind this memorial to the west lay Arlington National Cemetery and the stately Lee-Custis Mansion. Looking back toward the west, they again saw the Washington Monument and Capitol Hill. The city got closer as the plane continued its descent. They were over the runway when they heard the engines sound like they were slowing down, then the plane's wheels touched the runway, and the nose of the plane leveled off and touched down. The roar of the engines came alive once more as the captain put the brakes on behind the engines, and the plane began to slow down. After taxiing to its gate, the plane began to disembark its passengers. Hasan's face was one of seriousness and Ian and Abu still were not too sure of the reason for this trip. After collecting their bags from the overhead compartment, all three began to walk to the front of the plane. As they turned left to leave the plane, they saw the crew thank them for flying. The three continued to walk up the gate. As they entered the waiting area, Hasan, who was in front, began to look for Senator Chraft's driver. Hasan's eyes and those of Chraft's driver met as soon as he saw the sign the driver was holding with their names on it. He walked up to Chraft's assistant and introduced himself.

"I am Hasan. You must be Senator Chraft's driver?"

"Indeed, sir. Darrell Finch is the name. Very good to meet you."

Hasan introduced Darrell to Ian and Abu, and after exchanging greetings, Darrell told the three men he was instructed to take them immediately to the senator's office to meet with him.

"It's late; will the senator still be in his office?" Abu asked. He was Egyptian and had no understanding of American politics.

"The senator will indeed be in his office, Mr. Moustafa. He has a scheduled vote at ten this evening. He was hoping to meet with you three before he had to go to the senate and vote."

Darrell motioned for them to leave as it was already a quarter to eight and time was precious. On the way to Senator Chraft's office, all three took in the sights of Washington D.C. They once again passed the Lincoln Memorial.

The memorial was designed by Henry Bacon after ancient Greek temples. It stands one hundred feet high, one hundred nineteen feet wide and is one hundred and ninety feet long and is also surrounded by a peristyle of thirty-eight fluted Doric columns, each one standing for the thirty-six states in the Union at the time of his death. The north and south side chambers contain carved inscriptions of Lincoln's Second Inaugural and Gettysburg Address' respectively. The statue was carved in four years by the Piccirilli Brothers under the supervision of the sculptor, Daniel Chester French. Lincoln's statue itself is nineteen feet high and weighs in at one hundred and seventy-five tons. The original plan was for the statue to be ten feet high but that was changed so that the figure of Lincoln would not be dwarfed by the size of the chamber. A commission to plan the monument was first proposed in eighteen sixty-seven, shortly after his death. The design called for six equestrian and thirty-one pedestrian statues of colossal size, with a twelve-foot statue of Lincoln in the center, but that project was never completed due to lack of funding. Congress approved the bill to construct this memorial in nineteen-ten and work began in nineteen-fourteen. The memorial was opened to the public in nineteen-twenty-two and is also the site where civil rights leader Dr. Martin Luther King Jr. gave his "I Have a Dream" speech in nineteen-sixty-three. Off in the distance, they could see the Washington Monument. This monument was built between 1848 and 1884 as a memorial to George Washington. Its construction took place in two major phases; 1848–56 and 1876–1884 with the Civil War and a lack of funding causing the intermittent hiatus. Plans for a national monument began as early as 1783 when Major Peirre Charles L'Enfant proposed to Congress that an equestrian statue of the first president be erected. Although Congress authorized the monument, no action was taken by the time President Washington died in 1779. His death rekindled public aspiration for an appropriate memorial to him and John Marshall proposed that a special sepulcher be erected for the former General within the Capitol itself. Lack of funding postponed construction, but Marshall persevered and in 1883, he and James Madison formed the Washington National Monument Society. In 1836, the Society advertised for competitive architectural designs and the winning person was Robert Mills. His design called for a neoclassical plan that provided for a nearly flat-topped obelisk surrounded by a circular colonnade on which would stand a statue of Washington in a chariot. Inside the colonnade, statues of thirty prominent Revolutionary War heroes would be displayed. In 1858, the Civil War interrupted construction of the monument. When Lieutenant Colonel Thomas L. Casey, who was Robert Mills' successor, resumed the project in 1876, he redesigned the monument to resemble an unadorned Egyptian obelisk with a pointed pyramidion. The Corp of Engineers of the War Department was placed in charge of the final construction and the monument was dedicated on February 21st in 1885 and opened to the public on October 9th in 1888. The monument weighs in at 90,854 tons and stands 555 feet, 5 1/8th inches tall. A flight of 897 steps rises to the observation area in the pyramidion.[6]

"I love this place at night," Darrell said, interrupting their thoughts.

"If you look to the left, you can catch a glimpse of the White House."

The White House was well lit and beautiful. A little farther up Constitution Avenue North West, and they would reach their destination, the Russell Senate Building. Darrell parked the car, and he and his passengers got out. The building loomed large in front of them. The first congressional office buildings were constructed immediately after the turn of the century to receive overcrowding in the capitol. The prominent New York architectural firm of Carrere and Hastings was retained for construction in April 1904. Thomas Hastings oversaw the construction of the House Office building while John Carrere took charge of the Senate office building. The Russell building was occupied in 1909 by the Senate of the sixty-first Congress.[7] They walked in the door, got on the elevator, and Darrell pushed the button with the senator's name on it. The elevator doors closed, and the car began its ascent up to the senator's floor.

"The senator is looking very forward to meeting all of you. He wanted to me to extend to you his welcome and thanks for coming," Darrell said to the group. Ian and Abu exchanged indifferent glances.

"Thank you, Darrell," Hasan said, speaking on behalf of himself and Ian and Abu. The elevator stopped, the doors opened, and Darrell stepped out first.

"This way, gentlemen," he said waving his hand in the direction of the senator's office. The hallway was adorned with paintings of senators both past and present. The overhead lights were turned off and more quaint lighting adorning the walls was instead lit up, providing a more pleasurable ambience to the hallway.

Darrell noticed Abu looking at these lights. "Even in the Hart Senate Building, we have to find ways of saving energy," he said to Abu as they rounded a corner. "Last door on the left, gentlemen," he said walking past them so that he could knock on the senator's door, open it, and let them through in order to properly introduce them.

Darrell tapped softly but firmly on the door.

"Come in," came the voice from the other side. Darrell opened the door, stepped inside, and held the door open and waved the men in.

"Senator Clayton Chraft, may I present Drs. Ian James and Abu Moustafa. Dr. Habib you already know."

Clayton Chraft got up from behind his desk and walked toward the three men. Clayton Chraft was a tall man, six feet two inches, athletic build, steel gray eyes with the look of determination in them, and a full head of salt-and-pepper hair parted down the middle. He spoke with a deep but firm voice, yet his demeanor was that of a humble but passionate man. A pearly white smile flashed across his face, giving Ian and Abu the impression Clayton Chraft never met a stranger or anyone he didn't like.

"Gentlemen, welcome, thank you for coming," he said very enthusiastically. He shook each of their hands like someone who was ready to get down to business. He gave Hasan a hug and thanked him profusely. He also thanked Darrell for driving them from the airport. Darrell simply gave the senator a nod of his head.

"Gentlemen, can I get you anything to drink—soda, water, or perhaps a glass of wine?"

"Wine sounds good to me," Ian said.

"Me too," Abu acknowledged.

Darrell was at the bar pouring the respective drinks.

He also poured Hasan his favorite beverage—carbonated water. Hasan did not drink.

Ian and Abu each sat down in the two chairs in front of the senator's desk; Darrell and Hasan each sat in chairs next to the bar.

"The wine okay, gentlemen?" Clayton Chraft asked.

Both men raised their glasses and nodded their approval.

"I trust Hasan has told you why it was so imperative that I meet with you?"

"Something about an ark," Ian replied.

"Perfect," the senator said.

"Gentlemen," he continued, "do you believe in the God of the Bible?"

Ian took a long sip of wine and replied, "I grew up in church; my parents were both missionaries. I know the Bible very well, but I'm afraid I sort of got off the straight-and-narrow path. But to answer your question, Senator—"

The senator held his hand up. "Please, Ian, call me Clayton."

"To answer your question, Clayton, I'm a bit of an agnostic now. I believe in God, but would like some more proof."

"I am American born but I was raised in the culture of my native land, Egypt. My parents were Muslim, and they raised me in that religion. In Islam, we worship Allah; to Christians, he is God. To me, they are the same.

"Fair enough, gentlemen," Clayton said as he got up from behind his desk and walked around to the front of it.

He leaned back against his desk, rested both hands on either side of him, and he began his story.

"Ian, Abu, I have been absolutely fascinated by the epic of Noah and the ark as told in the book of Genesis since I was a young man. I have read everything I could ever get my hands on throughout the years. According to the book of Genesis, God told Noah to build the ark; Noah was six hundred years old at the time." Clayton Chraft reached in his desk and pulled a Bible from a drawer, turned to the book of Genesis, and began to read the sixth chapter, verses five through twenty-two to them. "God said to Noah, 'The end of all flesh is come before me; for the earth is filled with violence through them; and behold, I will destroy them with the earth. Make thee an ark of gopher wood; rooms shalt thou make in the ark, and shall pitch it within and without with pitch.'"

Ian, Abu, Darrell, and Hasan were listening intently to their boss. They knew of his passion to find the ark, but even they were surprised to see how excited he seemed.

Clayton Chraft, the son of William Chraft and whose grandfather started the family business and was now a United States senator, continued, "'A window shalt thou make to the ark, and in a cubit shalt thou finish it above. The length of the ark shall be three hundred cubits, and the breadth of it fifty cubits, and the height of it thirty cubits.'"

The more he spoke, the more of their attention he saw that he had.

"Then gentlemen, God said to Noah, 'And behold, I, even I, do bring a flood of waters upon the earth, to destroy all flesh, wherein is the breath of life, from under heaven; and everything that is in the earth shall die.'"

Time to reel them in, he thought.

"And then, my friends, God tells Noah that he will establish a covenant with him in that Noah and his family will be rescued from this cataclysmic worldwide flood by allowing Noah and his family a safe refuge on the ark. So, gentlemen, on December 7th—2,349 years before Christ was born—God commanded Noah and his family to enter the newly finished ark."

A look of amazement showed on Ian and Abu's faces.

Again, the senator continued, still leaning on his desk. "My friends, the eighth chapter of Genesis says the ark rested in the seventh month, on the seventeenth day of the month upon the mountains of Ararat. Ian, Abu, I believe that ark is still up there and I want you two, along with Hasan, to go up that mountain, locate and document the ark, and bring that information back to me," Clayton said as he walked toward the bar on the far side of his office. He poured himself a tall glass of sparkling water. He took a long drink, feeling the carbonation tickle his throat and the water soothe his thirst.

"Do any of you know exactly how big the ark was?"

Ian and Abu exchanged unsure glances. They had to admit to themselves and Clayton; they hadn't actually done the math.

"When finished, the ark measured four hundred fifty feet long, seventy-five feet wide, and forty-five feet high. Noah finished the ark to within eighteen inches of the top, where he installed a window. During construction, he also installed a door and made lower, middle, and upper decks. To put this in today's perspective, the ark had about one and half million cubic feet of free space, so the ark would have the equivalent volume of five hundred twenty-two American railroad stock cars, each of which could hold two hundred forty sheep."

CHAPTER 16

Hasan and Darrell stared at their boss. Abu sat silently pondering the information he had just heard. Ian stood to his feet, turned to face Clayton Chraft, drained the wine from his glass, and gave the senator a look that said, *do you expect me to believe this?*

"What about all those animals, Clayton? Do you really believe all those animals could fit on that boat?" Ian asked, looking for any reason the senator would begin to doubt himself.

Clayton Chraft fired back his answer very confidently. "My faith is intact, Dr. James. The Bible says the ark is on Mount Ararat; therefore, I believe it. I am not interested in the animal-to-ark ratio. I want to pay you and your associates to go up that mountain, take pictures, make drawings and documentations of that ark until there is nothing left to document, and I want you to bring it all back here to me. There have been numerous expeditions up that mountain in the past because people have believed there was something up there.

"For instance, in 1877, Prince John Joseph of Nouri was said to have found Noah's ark on Mount Ararat. In 1893, he stated his intention to organize an expedition to dissemble the ark and reassemble it for the Chicago World's Fair. He applied for a Turkish permit to accomplish this, but the government turned him down. Twenty-nine years later, in 1916, several Turkish soldiers reportedly stumbled upon a large damaged wooden ship, which coincidently was in the general vicinity of the anomaly photographed by the Pentagon in its 1949 aerial mission. In the summer of 1916, a large Russian military expedition supposedly examined the ark after one of their pilots claimed to have discovered it accidentally while testing a new high-altitude engine. On July fifth, 1955, a French industrialist and explorer named Ferdinand Navarra made history when he became the first person in modern times to find a five-foot piece of ancient, hand-crafted wood on Mount Ararat some forty feet under the Parrot Glacier on the northwest slope."

Clayton put a hand on both Ian's shoulders to drive home his point with a smile on his face.

"Don't you see, Ian? There have been far too many occurrences of people sighting the ark. In the late fifteenth century, Marco Polo, on his way to China, made mention in his *Travels of Marco Polo* that the ark was still visible on top of Ararat. A young boy named George Hagopian wrote of his father taking him up the mountain to play on the ark. George was a ten-year-old boy in 1905. He said that the ark was totally intact. So you see, Ian and Abu that I am passionate about the ark and my faith that it does exist."

Clayton took his hands from off Ian's shoulders and returned to his desk and sat back down.

"But Clayton, if the Turkish government refused to

let Prince John Joseph of Nouri go up the mountain, what makes you think they would give us permission to do so?" Abu asked, beginning to digest the information Clayton had just talked about. Although Abu was Egyptian, he had no idea there been so many sightings and so many people interested in finding the ark.

"Money will buy cooperation, Abu. My last name is Chraft and my family is worth billions. I purposed in my heart long ago that I would do whatever it takes to find the ark, even it meant spending my entire family fortune."

"How is that going over with your family, Clayton?" Abu asked, wanting to see just how serious the senator was about finding the ark and spending his family's fortune in the process.

Clayton looked piercingly into Abu's eyes and said, "Some of them support my idea, others aren't so sure, but they are my family nevertheless.

At that point, Clayton Chraft's phone rang on his desk. He pushed the button to put the person on the other end of the line on the speaker.

"Yes?" he answered.

"Sorry, old buddy, but your vote on keeping the phrase 'under God' in the pledge of allegiance won't be needed tonight. Seems our esteemed colleague from Utah doesn't like the wording on the bill, so it's being held up. Better luck tomorrow."

"Okay, Tom, thanks."

Clayton shook his head. *That senator from Utah,* he thought to himself.

Now Clayton was more determined than ever.

"Gentlemen, this is also why I want to find the ark; the esteemed colleague my associate Tom was referring to is another senator whose constituent is a very wealthy organization called the American Civil Liberties Union. This organization is trying its best to erase God from our society. If you go to Ararat, find and document the ark and bring that proof back to me and I will use that to prove them wrong. With that kind of physical proof, the American Civil Liberties Union will no longer have a leg to stand on. Dr. James, Dr. Moustafa, will you please help me? I have rooms reserved for you at the Washington Hilton, which is only a few blocks from here. Darrell will take you there now. Go to your rooms and think about my offer to both of you. Abu, I would love to see you as your own boss in your new museum and use the five million to do with as you please. Ian, I'm also quite sure you too could play with five million dollars, and I can make arrangements for you to be my chief archeologist on the expedition I also have planned to find the Ten Commandments, but one thing at a time. Be warned; my esteemed colleague from Utah also knows of my desire to find the ark, he does not want this to happen, and he too has people who work for him to see that finding the ark does not happen. But Ian and Abu, I promise I will make this worth your while."

"I told Hasan I can't cash a promise, Senator. How do we know you won't go back on this promise of yours?" Ian asked matter-of-factly.

"Dr. James, I hope you will be able to trust me enough to take my word for it. I have poured my thoughts out to you for the past hour and a half, and I have also made known to you what I want to do. I realize you know me only through Dr. Habib, but I also trust he was able to give you both a good sense about me—a 'warm fuzzy' if you will. Gentlemen, go back to the hotel and take the rest of the night to think about it and let me know your decision tomorrow. It's late, and you need your rest after your long trip," Clayton Chraft said as he checked his watch. The three men got up to leave, and Darrell escorted them out. They bid Senator Chraft good night as they all shook hands and left.

The three were all silent as they walked back down the hallway toward the elevator. Hasan looked at Abu and Ian for any signs of interest as they felt the elevator slowly come to a halt on the first floor. It looked as if his friends had their poker faces on as he saw no signs of anything that looked like interest as they felt the elevator slowly come to a halt on the first floor. Darrell checked his watch, he let out an uncomfortable sigh as it was well past midnight and he still had to drive these men to their hotel and make sure they got checked in okay. He still had the thirty-minute drive back to his apartment in the Washington D.C. suburb of Alexandria. He had to get up at 5 a.m. to begin his day of running errands for the senator, and he was already exhausted.

The elevator stopped, and the doors opened. Ian stepped out first, and they walked to the front doors of the lobby. The men walked outside to the senator's limousine, and they climbed inside.

"Gentlemen, I'll take you to the hotel now, and I will

be back to pick you up at 7:00 a.m. to bring you back to talk to Senator Chraft," Darrell said as he attempted to start anything that sounded like a casual conversation. His words fell on deaf ears as everyone was lost in their own thoughts. He turned the key to the ignition, and the engine came to life. The hotel was only a fifteen-minute drive away, but it was going to be a long one.

The limousine pulled up to the front doors of the hotel, and Ian, Abu, and Hasan all climbed out of the car. Darrell watched as they walked into the lobby and up to the front desk. Abu checked with the concierge for a reservation of three rooms under Carlton Chraft's name. The concierge told them they did, and he would have the bellboy take their luggage up to their rooms.

Hasan turned to Darrell, who was still waiting in the limo, and gave him the thumbs up sign that they were indeed checked in. Darrell waved back as he began his drive home to his place. Darrell knew how passionate his boss was about the ark of Noah and hoped himself that these men would agree to go to Mount Ararat and find the ark. He turned on the radio to keep himself company.

Chapter 17

The elevator doors opened, and the bellboy led the way out with their suitcases on a dolly. He stopped in front of Ian's room and ran his card through the electronic slot. The door buzzed, and John, the bellboy, went in. He showed Ian where the bathroom was and told him if he needed anything to simply call the front desk for service. Ian tipped him, and John waved for the other two men to follow him back out into the hallway. John then showed Abu and Hasan their respective rooms where he also went through the same routine with them. Both men tipped John, who went back out into the hallway and down the elevator. Ian went out of his room and into the hallway where he met Abu. They looked at each other and without saying anything looked at Hasan's door. Abu was the first to knock on the door. It opened, and Abu walked in with Ian trailing behind. The door closed, and Ian was first to speak.

"Senator Chraft is serious; I'll give him that much," he said as he walked to Hasan's refrigerator and grabbed a bottle of sparkling water.

"I told you on the flight over here that he was. He is very serious about this, and the both of you must come to an agreement that you will do this," Hasan said, arms crossed and looking very serious himself.

"Five million dollars is a lot of money, and the things I could do with that amount—" Ian replied as he stroked his chin in an outward thought.

"I could do a lot of things for the museum. I have wanted to expand it, as there is—"

The men's conversation was interrupted by a knock on the door.

"Who is it?" Hasan asked, as it was now past one o'clock in the morning.

"Room service," came the reply from the other side of the door.

"I did not order anything," Hasan answered back cautiously. He glanced at his colleagues, and both of them shook their heads no.

"No, thank you," He shot back.

"A gift from Senator Chraft, sir. He didn't think you had a chance to eat, and he ordered some lobster and shrimp to be sent up. It's very delicious, sir."

Hasan looked through the peephole of his door, and there stood John the bellboy with a large platter on a dolly. He looked back at his friends and nodded that it was indeed room service.

"Room service; at least we're not paying for it," Abu said as he nodded for Hasan to open the door and let John in.

Hasan opened the door only slightly, and in burst four men, who were all carrying guns. The first one went up to Ian and punched him in the jaw, knocking him down and his bottle of water flew out of his hand and splattered against the wall. The other two men put their guns against the abdomens of Abu and Hasan without saying a word. The fourth man nodded his approval.

"I think these boys all get the point." He stepped aside and in walked Montgomery James Swanson III, the distinguished gentleman from the state of Utah. Ian instantly knew they had been setup. He was also a bit groggy from the sucker punch the senator's ruffian gave him upon entering the room. He picked himself up from the floor as Monty approached him.

"So, you're the ring leader of this outfit, huh?" he asked Ian rather sarcastically. Ian said nothing as he wiped the blood from his lower lip with the back of his right hand. Senator Swanson casually walked around the suite Senator Chraft had reserved for Hasan.

"You would think that man would've got you boys a much better room with the money he has," Monty commented as he ran his fingers along the large windowsill.

Hasan watched him while he talked. He knew he had better not fight back, as these men had guns, and neither he nor Ian or Abu had one. He wanted to fight back, but common sense dictated otherwise.

"Should we work them over, Boss? Sort of drive the point home a little more I think," the first henchman said as he stared into Ian's face. It had been some time since he was in a position to push his weight around, and he wanted to fight.

"No, that won't be necessary. If these boys don't think

I mean business with guns pointed at them, they're stupid. And we both know you're not stupid, don't we, Dr. James?" Monty quipped as he again approached Ian.

"No, I think by the look on Dr. James's face he knows he has a much better decision to make." Monty turned and walked across the room to take a seat on the couch.

"Boys, come over here and have a seat; we've got some business to attend to."

Senator Swanson's men motioned with their guns for Ian, Abu, and Hasan to have a seat.

Hasan was more cautious than scared; Abu was not quite sure what to think of this situation, and Ian looked at his assailant's face as the gun motioned for him to move. All three sat down, a nervous look coming over their collective faces.

Monty leaned forward, resting his elbows on his knees; he interlocked his fingers together.

"Dr. James, Dr. Moustafa, Dr. Habib, I'll get right to the point," he said as he looked at each of them.

"I know exactly why Clayton Chraft wants to send you on this little trip to Ararat; he wants you three to up that mountain and find Noah's ark. Now, assuming you believe that boat is still up there, and assuming you even remotely believe in what the Bible says about it, do you boys honestly think you will even make it up there? But you know what? Let's pretend it is up there. What of it? What's going to happen next in the world? I'll tell you what will happen: absolutely nothing—that's what. The only thing that's going to happen is the media will report on it, which will last a few days, and then they and the rest of the world will move on. You'll all get your name in the papers, the media will mention your names a few times and that's it. Besides, gentlemen, let's even assume you make it up that mountain. Does Clayton Chraft have enough money to pay off the warLORDs operating in that area? Do you really think that man will pay you the money he has promised to each of you? Remember, the man is a politician first, a businessman second. The man is rich, but do you really think his family is going to let him pay each of you the money? Think about it, boys, even though he comes from money, do you really think his family will let him go through with this? I know about his family, and I can tell you they did not get rich by sending people on wild goose chases like this. But let's assume you do go; as I said before, what makes you think you'll get up that mountain? What makes you even think you will make it to Turkey? Dr., James, Dr. Moustafa,Dr. Habib, what makes you think you'll even make it to the airport?" James said as he pointed to all three of them.

"How about we do this: You guys stay for the night, enjoy yourselves. Tomorrow I will drop by and talk to you." Ian looked at his watch.

"It's two o'clock. I'll be back here at nine tomorrow morning to make sure you all made the right decisions."

As Montgomery James Swanson III got up to exit the suite, his first henchman drove his right fist into the left side of Ian's face, knocking him into Abu's lap.

"Please, we get the point!" Abu exclaimed throwing his hand up to ward off any further attacks.

"Nine o'clock, guys," the man said before turning to exit the suite.

Ian raised himself from Abu's lap.

"Are you okay, my friend?" he asked, looking at Ian's left cheekbone that was already starting to bruise.

"Yeah, I'll live, but I'll tell you both one thing: we're not staying here another minute," he said, getting up to check his face and put some ice on it.

Hasan got up to look out the suite window. On the street below, he saw Senator Swanson and his men get into a black Dodge sport utility vehicle with government license plates on it and drive away.

"He is gone," Hasan announced, not looking away from the window.

"You guys okay?" all three of them turned to see John standing by the wet bar. In all the commotion, they had forgotten he was still there.

"Yeah, we're okay, but why are you still here?" Hasan asked, rather surprised.

"I had a gun on me, too," John answered back.

"Are you sure they're gone?" he asked Hasan.

"Yes, I can't see anyone standing around down there trying to look inconspicuous," he answered.

"Good," John replied. He took out his cell phone. All three men looked at him curiously.

"Darrell, John here. I need you to come back to the hotel and pick these guys up. You'll be here in fifteen minutes? See you then. We'll be down in the lobby in five. Meet me in back of the hotel." He pushed a button to hang up the phone.

"You work for Senator Chraft too?" Abu asked John in an amazed tone.

"Let's just say Clayton Chraft has people," John answered.

I'll never understand American politics, Abu thought to himself. *First, there was coming to America to meet with Senator Chraft. Second, there was all the talk about going to Ararat and finding Noah's ark. The final insult was being manhandled by Monty's ruffians. What's next?* "Leaving for Turkey," Hasan answered his friend as he saw the look on Abu's face.

"What airline does the senator have us on, and what time does it leave?" Hasan turned and asked John.

"Air Canada, and it leaves from Ronald Reagan National Airport at nine. Your plane will fly straight from there all the way to Ankara," John answered him.

"We need to get downstairs immediately and get you guys out of the hotel. Time, gentlemen, is of the essence. You can change your clothes and rest after you arrive and meet with the senator's contact he has there," he continued.

"Let's get out of here," Abu said as he headed out the door, Ian, Hasan and John all trailing him.

While they are walking down the hallway toward the elevator, Hasan called the senator to let him know that they were on the way out of the hotel and to the airport. The senator told him that there would be a contact in the lobby to ensure they got out without being seen.

As they exited the elevator, they saw their contact; he was acting like a customer who was not happy with the service of the hotel. He was busily arguing with one of Swanson's men. Swanson's henchman was trying his level best to let this guy know that he did not work for the hotel.

While this was going on, another one of Chraft's contacts turned his head in the direction the men should go. They walked past the henchman as his back was turned to them. They walked down the hallway to the hotel bar, where another contact of Chraft told them to come behind the counter, through the stockroom, and out the back door. They exited the door to a waiting car parked in the lot. They climbed in, and Darrell pulled out, heading toward Ronald Reagan National Airport.

"Guys, I have been instructed to tell you that Chraft has deposited half of your monies into your accounts. He also says thank you for doing this."

As he was telling them this, another car pulled out, and its headlights came on.

Darrell saw the car in his side view mirror, and he also checked his rearview.

"We got company!" he exclaimed. He floored the gas pedal, trying to put distance between them and the trailing car. It sped up and plowed into the back of Darrell's car, denting the back bumper and pushing it forward.

"Hold on!" Darrell told them. They were going way above the speed limit, but in this case, it was a necessity.

The trailing car followed suit, and the situation became a full-fledged car chase.

Senator Swanson's driver got into the passing lane and pulled up next to Darrell, swerving to the right in an attempt to knock them off the road. Darrell compensated and, in return, swerved to the left to knock the other car off the street. There was very little traffic this early in the morning. He hoped he could get them to the airport without getting into an accident.

Mahmood's partner, Jim, the first man to enter Abu's room and punch Ian in the face, told him to pull up beside the other car so that he could shoot Darrell.

Jim screwed the silencer onto the end of the gun he was using; Mahmood pulled up beside Darrell's car, and the passenger aimed his gun at Darrell.

"Get down!" Darrell shouted, and everyone buried themselves in the seats.

Jim got two shots off as Darrell made a hard left swerve, hitting Mahmood's car very hard and knocking the gun out of Jim's hand.

Senator Swanson's henchmen sideswiped them again, and Ian instantly recognized the driver of the other car—it was Mahmood. Ian's mind raced back to the pharaoh's tomb entrance, and he remembered Mahmood being there.

"It's Mahmood!" he stated.

"Who?" Hasan asked impatiently.

"Mahmood. He was dressed as a security guard at the pharaoh's tomb back in Egypt. The security agency Abu called had no record of anyone new being hired when we found out he should not have been there. He's driving the other car!"

Mahmood swerved sharply to the right again, attempting to knock Ian off the road. In retaliation,

Darrell steered hard left, sideswiping Mahmood's car. He lost control and slammed into a parked car head on. His driver side airbag deployed on impact as both cars were destroyed.

Darrell continued to race toward the airport, but at a slower speed than before so as to not attract any unwanted attention.

Mahmood was dazed and shaken. He felt warmth running down his nose. He wiped his upper lip and looked at his hand; it was full of blood. He realized his nose was busted. He shakily turned to his partner who was staring at him. Jim was staring at back at him with an empty gaze.

He realized his partner's neck was broken due to the strange angle of his neck. He knew his partner was dead. He stumbled out of the car and called his boss to explain to him what just happened. Swanson told him to get the mess cleaned up and get back to his office. He found a phone number on his cell and pushed the call button, and within a few minutes a tow truck, driven by another one of Swanson's men, pulled up and put the destroyed car on its flatbed. Another car arrived, and he got into the car. The driver helped get Jim's body into the car, and they began to make the trip back to the senator's office. But first, a little side trip was in order to get rid of the body occupying the backseat along with him.

CHAPTER 18

Dawn broke as Darrell pulled into the parking lot of Ronald Reagan National Airport. He parked in the slot marked "Government Vehicles Only," and the four men piled out of the car quickly.

"We need to hurry; your flight leaves at nine!" Darrell told them as they hurried toward the ticket counter. The counters were all packed with passengers who also had early-morning flights. After what seemed like an eternity, the ticket lady motioned for Darrell to come up and be served.

"Ma'am, all these guys are booked on the same flight to Ankara, Turkey."

"All right, sir, may I see your photo identification please?" she said to Hasan.

He put out his driver's license and showed it to the lady.

"Window or aisle seat, sir?" she asked him

"I don't really care, ma'am," he replied in return.

She gave him an aisle seat, and with the click of the mouse, a printer produced his boarding pass.

"Are you claiming any baggage, sir?" she asked.

"No, I am traveling light today," he replied, trying to

be courteous. Hasan was very ready to get on the plane and get this trip started.

Ian was next and went through the same routine with the lady, as did Abu.

Soon, the four of them were scurrying to the security checkpoint. The line was long, but it looked like it would be quick. Right before Darrell and John left them, John gave them further instructions.

"A man the senator has paid will meet you at the airport. His name is Adnan. He will be holding a sign with Hasan's name on it."

He turned to talk to Hasan specifically. "You will then introduce these two, and Adnan will take you to his cab, then on to the hotel. All of you will then get some rest. Senator Chraft will call you the next morning and let you know who your contacts are so that you can get to Ararat."

All of them nodded that they understood John's instructions.

"We wish you all the best of luck," John and Darrell told them as they each shook hands and before Ian, Abu, and Hasan walked through the metal detector.

"Sir, without a boarding pass, this is as far as you may go," the security guard told John, who let her know that he was just saying goodbye to his friends.

Ian and the other two hurried to their gate. The flight left in one hour.

Chapter 19

"Did you boys get the mess cleaned up?" Swanson asked as Mahmood walked into the office and made his way toward the couch that sat along the wall opposite the senator's desk.

"We got it cleaned up, Boss, and Jim's body will never be found. The car is sitting outside the gate of a junkyard out of town, and by now, I'm sure there is one angry owner of a completely destroyed car that looked like it was brand new. I sure hope they had insurance," Tyler Newsome replied to his uncle Swanson. His mother, Mary Newsome, was Monty's kid sister. She was the youngest of four siblings, and he brought Tyler in to work for him running errands—whatever those errands might be.

"You okay, Mahmood?" Monty finally managed to ask, walking over to the couch to get a closer look at his nose.

"I'll be okay, Boss. Jim is worse off than me," he answered.

"Yeah, it's a doggone shame about him. But that's life, or death in his case," Monty replied. Mahmood shot Swanson a nasty look but knew there was nothing else he could do. Couldn't Monty at least have just a bit more compassion?

"How far are we behind those boys?" Swanson asked his nephew.

"At least twelve hours. The next flight to Ankara leaves tonight at nine," he answered his uncle.

"What airline did they fly out on, out of which airport?" Monty asked his young, ambitious nephew.

"Air Canada, and out of Reagan National Airport," Tyler answered.

"Okay, book a flight for you and Mahmood for tonight. Chraft thinks he's the only one with connections; well, I know some people too. I'll make a couple of phone calls, and in the meantime, both of you go home and try to get some rest. I'll call you later," Monty said to Tyler.

Monty turned to Mahmood. "You sure you're all right, buddy?"

Mahmood stood to his feet and looked his boss in the eye.

"I'll be fine; it's just a busted nose. I'll go home and take a couple of aspirin then go to bed," he replied back to the senator. His mind was still reeling from the crash that also killed Jim. He and Jim had worked together on many other "errands," and both knew they could count on each other and became good friends. Couldn't this schmuck, whose name was Swanson and who also was an heir to the Swanson Insurance fortune, and just as Senator Chraft, who also stood to inherit his money as well, have just a smidgen of anything that looked a lot like compassion?

Either one is born a schmuck, or the money one stands

to inherit makes you one. Or maybe it was a little of both. Mahmood couldn't decide on the correct answer.

Either way, it didn't seem to make a difference with Montgomery James Swanson III, the distinguished gentleman who lost one of his men in a car crash only a few hours before.

Mahmood knew that if the situation called for it, he could and had to be the "heavy" at times. But this time, it involved the death of his friend and coworker. He did not like that one bit.

"Mahmood, shrug it off. I'll take you home. You pour yourself a shot of some of that Egyptian whiskey you let me taste the last time I was at your place. It'll calm your nerves, and besides, we both need your head in the game for what we are about to do. Come on. I'll take you home."

He took a deep breath and shook his head, trying to recollect his thoughts. He cocked his chin to let Tyler know he was ready to go. Tyler forked his pinky finger and thumb to his head and mouthed the words "call me later" to his uncle, who nodded that he would.

Tyler patted Mahmood on the back as they exited Monty's office.

Monty pushed the call button on his phone. "Gwen, cancel all my appointments today. I have some personal business I have to attend to instead."

"Yes, Mr. Swanson," Gwen answered.

He did not like the look in Mahmood's eyes; that look seemed to be full of defiance. Monty was not one to be talked back to in such a manner. He was the kind of man who was used to getting his own way, and whatever he said was how things were going to be, period.

At least that means that Mahmood still has a lot of spunk, Monty thought to himself. *He'll need that where he is going, and besides, Mahmood knows how to get the job done.*

Monty sat down at his desk and clicked the computer mouse on the "ark" icon on his desktop.

Thcy were still there, photos of Noah's ark from past expeditions. He clicked out of the picture file on his computer. He turned it off and got up to put his suit jacket on and leaves his office for home. He was tired and needed sleep; after all, it had been a very long night.

Chapter 20

"We've got to get to C-12 as fast as we can; the flight leaves in forty-five minutes," Hasan told his colleagues as they walked briskly in the direction of their gate. The excitement was starting to build inside him. It was only a few days ago that they were in Abu's apartment and he was in the process of talking these guys into jumping on a plane and flying to Washington D.C. to meet with Senator Chraft. The meeting went rather well, and Chraft sold the importance, urgency, and necessity of going to Ararat to document the ark. And the financial incentives were good to. Five million apiece for Abu and Ian—Abu, who wanted to be curator of his own museum, and Ian, whom Chraft was going to make chief archeologist of the senator's next big find. What that might be was unknown at this time, but first things first.

"It's up there to the right!" Abu said as they were nearing the departure gate. The line was long; this was going to be a full flight.

"Checking in, ma'am," Ian said to the counter person. "These guys are with me as well," he added, motioning to the two men standing next to him.

She looked at all their boarding passes and informed

them they were all set. Boarding would begin in fifteen minutes. For the first time since they were handed their tickets, Ian looked at his.

At least they're first class, he thought to himself.

He thought they had rather nice hotel suites, even though Senator Quigley disagreed.

Now, they each had first-class tickets. What could be better than that?

"Ladies and gentlemen, we do welcome you onboard flight nineteen sixty-three with non-stop service to Ankara, Turkey. We will now board all first-class passengers and those with special needs or those needing assistance," the lady's voice said, coming across the gates intercom.

Being boarded first is good too, Ian thought to himself.

Hasan handed the lady his ticket; she gave him back his boarding pass. Ian and Abu followed suit, and each man made his way down the ramp toward the waiting plane. They found their respective seats, sat down, and got settled in. In a matter of minutes, the plane was fully loaded, and the flight attendants were giving their safety briefing. While this was going on, the plane was backed away from the gate and the engines came to life as the plane began its short trip to the beginning of the runway. As the plane took its spot on the tarmac, the engines were turned up to full power. The passengers could feel themselves sinking into their seats as the plane gained speed further down the runway. The nose led skyward as it was now airborne and on its way to Turkey. Flight nineteen sixty-three attained cruising altitude and breakfast was served. The three men ate heartily, and within minutes, exhaustion crept over each of them.

They hadn't slept in a little over forty-eight hours, and now it was time for rest. Ian, Abu, and Hasan put a pillow beside their heads and settled in for the long twelve-hour flight. They were asleep within minutes.

CHAPTER 21

Tyler was startled from his sleep by the sound of his cell phone ringing. He had laid it on the nightstand by his bed before he lay down. He picked it up to see who was calling. His uncle's name appeared on the small screen.

"Hello?" he said into the tiny handset in a very sleepy voice.

"It's six p.m. Time to get up, shower, and get ready for your flight," Uncle Swanson replied back to him.

"Okay, I'm getting up now. Have you called Mahmood yet, or should I do it?"

"He's on his way over to pick you up. I called him first. I don't think he got much sleep; in fact, I don't think he slept at all. Probably still upset about last night, but he'll get over it. In my line of work, you got to make sacrifices sometimes."

"Did he sound angry when you called him?"

"He sounded tired and somewhat upset, maybe even a little hung over, but he can sleep it off on the plane. Anyway, don't worry about Mahmood; he'll be fine. You get your butt up and get dressed. You got a long flight ahead of you."

By this time, Tyler was already up and about to take

a shower. He was laying his clothes out when his door buzzer sounded.

"Uncle Monty, Mahmood just rang the buzzer. I got to and let him in. I'll call you from the airport after we get to our gate."

"You do that. Oh, by the way, I called my contact in Ankara. Everything has been taken care of. All you have to do is get there and take care of business."

"Understood," Tyler said as he hung up the phone and let Mahmood in. Tyler closed the door behind him.

"You okay, Mahmood?" Tyler asked him.

"I will be fine. Let's hurry; we have many things to do."

He replied, turning to Tyler to answer his question. If Mahmood was angry, upset, or a little hung over, Tyler could not tell. What he could tell was that Mahmood was all about business and that was a good thing.

"Give me fifteen minutes to get showered and dressed, and then we'll be on our way."

Tyler said, motioning for Mahmood to sit down. He held his hand up; he did not feel like sitting down. Tyler left to take his shower.

Mahmood strolled around the apartment. "Nice place, would your mother be proud of you now?" he said under his breath.

On this wall there was a nice family photo of Tyler and his parents. His father was dressed very casually in a Hawaiian shirt and shorts; his mom was dressed in a two-piece bikini with a sheer scarf wrapped around her waist.

Tyler was sitting down between them; his mother's hands rested on his shoulders, his dad's hands rested on hers.

"Springbreak my senior year at Harvard," Tyler said as Mahmood turned in the direction of his voice. Tyler was dressed in pleated slacks and a blue shirt, his carry-on luggage swung over his shoulder and his sunglasses resting on top of his head. Mahmood had an *are you kidding me?* Look on his face.

"Hey man, I believe in looking good no matter where I go," he said with a smile on his face.

They both headed for the door.

Chapter 22

"Ladies and gentlemen, please bring your seats to the upright position and fold your tables up; we are thirty minutes from landing. Local time is eight thirty p.m., and the weather is clear. Temperature is a nice eighty-five degrees. Flight attendants please cross check," the captain's voice coming over the intercom said. All three came awake at this time.

I need coffee, Ian thought to himself. Abu was getting a good stretch in. Hasan dialed Senator Chraft's cell phone number. He told Chraft that they were thirty minutes from landing. Chraft told Hasan that his contacts would be waiting for them when they landed. He also informed Hasan that their contacts were a local businessman and his associates. He informed Hasan that he knew them through Hasan's cousin, who drove a city taxi. They landed at Ankara, Turkey's Esenboga Airport. The plane taxied to its inbound terminal. After it came to a stop, the captain turned off the fasten seatbelt sign. The passengers rose from their seats and opened the overhead compartments in search of their carry-on luggage that was just a little too big to fit under their seats. The three men got in line and began to follow the other first-class passengers off the plane. They disembarked and made their way to baggage claim. Even though they had no luggage, this was also the way out of the airport.

Outside the baggage terminal, there was no one to pick them up. Each of their eyes began to scan the crowd outside, but they found no one.

"This is not good!" Hasan exclaimed.

Abu and Ian both looked at him as if to say, *Now what?*

Hasan opened his cell phone and called Clayton Chraft. He was told that the senator's contacts and his cousin had been killed overnight and dumped into a river. Chraft told Hasan that he was watching the news and they were reporting it now. Hasan was told to get something to eat and that he would get another phone call in one hour. He hailed a taxi, and the three got in. The taxi driver was told to take them to a restaurant. The taxi driver pulled away from the curb and turned the meter on. He asked them where they wanted to go and Hasan told him to find the nearest restaurant as it didn't matter what kind of food they were going to eat. He had lost his appetite at the news of his cousin's death but they couldn't stay at the airport terminal waiting for a phone call that was coming an hour from now.

CHAPTER 23

"We just got through airport security, and we're on our way to the gate. Our flight takes off in one hour," Tyler told his uncle Swanson. Both he and Mahmood had their carry-ons strapped over their shoulders, and both were also scurrying though the airport to get to their terminal.

"That's good, boys. Fortunately, about this time, those boys have discovered that things didn't go as planned for them. It seems their ride couldn't quite make it to the airport to pick them up, seems they were disposed of sometime during the night and their bodies dumped in the river," Swanson explained to Tyler. Mahmood pointed to their gate in the distance.

"Fast and efficient work on their part it seems," Tyler replied back to his uncle.

"They're a bunch of good boys." Monty said to his nephew before taking another sip of his drink.

"We're at our gate. Plane leaves in forty-five minutes. I'll call you when we land," Tyler replied.

"Now listen, when you land, go rent a car. I got you booked in a hotel right across the street from the airport. Call me when you both get checked in. We'll talk more at that time," Swanson informed his nephew. He was more than glad he brought his forty-five-year-old nephew into his fold. Tyler was not only ambitious and smart, but he was also cut from the same mold as his uncle was. Monty Swanson definitely had plans for his young nephew. Monty hung up the phone and dialed his colleague Senator Quigley's number.

James picked up the phone.

"Monty, it's about time you called. I was beginning to think you'd forgotten about us," James said into the phone without saying hello first. Monty's name appeared on his cell phone screen.

"Calm yourself, Jim. Everything's fine. We need to have a meeting tonight at the office so I can bring you and the boys up to speed on what's been happening in the past seventy-two hours."

"What time do you want to hold the meeting, Monty?"

"How about ten o'clock at the office?"

"Mine or yours?"

"No, James, *the* office," Monty said with a little laugh.

"I see, you want to hold the meeting in the ACLU boardroom tonight," James replied.

"Sure do. Listen, old buddy, do me a favor and call everyone else in as well. I think you'll all get a kick out of what I have to say."

"Will do my friend. I'll make some phone calls, and we'll see you at ten."

Monty hung up the phone. He looked at the view outside his third-story office window and felt very proud of himself. It had been a good day.

CHAPTER 24

The taxi driver dropped Ian, Abu, and Hasan off at a restaurant about fifteen minutes from the airport. Hasan's mind was reeling. One of his cousins was dead and so were Chraft's contacts. They found a table in the corner of the restaurant, and the waiter brought them menus. He asked them if they would like something to drink. They all agreed on coffee, and he left to get them something to keep them awake.

"Someone does not want us to get to Ararat," Abu said as the waiter returned with the coffee.

"I hope Chraft finds out who did this. This makes no sense!" Hasan exclaimed to his friends. Although he made his home in the United States, he was still very close to his family in Turkey.

"I think we need to hear back from Chraft before any revenge is taken on anyone," Ian said to Hasan, leaning in close to his friend and looking into his eyes to get his point across.

The waiter returned to ask them if they were ready to order. His English was broken but passable. They asked for a little more time, realizing they had not looked at the menu.

"How can we possibly eat at a time such as this? My cousin's body had been floating in the river for hours until he was found. And now here I am sitting in this place waiting for something to eat. I should be with my family mourning his death," Hasan said, hanging his head as he spoke those last words.

"Hasan, maybe the best way to mourn his death is to find the ark," Abu said to him, trying to make sense of all this.

"The ark, the ark. You speak of something that no one is even sure exists. Just because Chraft sincerely believes it's up there, and because I have been working for him for so long, I am sitting here instead of mourning my family's loss. I should not be here. I should be with them!" he retorted. His sense of guilt, anger, and pain showed obviously on his face.

"My friend, again I suggest that finding the ark is the best way to honor your cousin's memory. It is not his or your fault that he was in the wrong place at the wrong time—"

"Chraft put him in the wrong place at the wrong time!" Hasan exclaimed, pointing his finger at Abu in an attempt to justify his claim. Ian looked around the restaurant and saw they were starting to attract attention.

"Gentlemen, relax. Hasan, you need to realize that your cousin agreed to pick us up from the airport. Did that put him in the wrong place at the wrong time? Maybe yes, maybe no, but he willingly did it. Not only for you, but for us too. Plus, when you started talking about how sincerely Chraft believes in this, you forgot one very important thing—you accepted payment for this. Now, I agree with Abu on something—that maybe finding the ark is the only honorable way for you to mourn and avenge his death. And there is also one other thing, what else can we do, except to sit here and wait for Chraft to call," Ian told Hasan, trying to be both firm but also gentle at the same time. It was going to take Hasan some time to get his head around this.

"Ready, gentlemen?" The waiter asked, pen and paper in hand.

Somewhere in the back of his mind, Hasan knew Abu and Ian were both right. His anger was such that it clouded his thinking. Hasan had come from a large family and they were all very close to one another. He remembered in his youth how, on Friday evenings, at the beginning of the Sabbath, the entire family would gather at his paternal grandparents' house for the weekly feast. The feast would rotate each week: one week at a grandparent's house, next week at cousin's house, and so it went until he was in his early twenties.

Hasan moved to America at that time to go to school to learn how to be a chef. This was the desire of his father, who took over the family restaurant business from his father. Hasan's father knew that in order for the restaurant to stay competitive, they would have to start serving more Westernized dishes—something Grandfather opposed. In order for Hasan to begin preparation to take over the family business, he needed to know how to cook more modernized foods. But unfortunately for him, he had a temper, and every time the head chef tried to correct him on how to prepare Western cuisines, his temper got in his way. At first, without telling his father, he dropped out of culinary school. However, his father soon learned that his son was no longer going to school.

After a heated argument on the phone, his father told him he would return to school because it was his father's intent for Hasan to take over the family business. He told his father he would have no part of the restaurant and that he had his own dreams to follow. Father replied back with his own ultimatum: "Go back to school, take over the restaurant, and move back home, or the checks that are paying your rent and tuition will cease to come in the mail. And if you do not do as I wish, I will disown you as my son." Hasan could not believe his ears, but knew he had to follow his heart. His father hung up on him. His mother had died when he was young, and since he had inherited his temper from his father, there was no one to talk sense into him once father's mind was made up. That's all there was to it.

Over the years, he did keep in touch with his aunt, uncles, and cousins. He would often inquire about his father but was told that each time the subject was brought up that his father would either change the subject or leave. Hasan sorely missed his father, and the letters he wrote and the e-mails he sent to him continued to go unanswered. Finally, after years of trying to reconcile with his father, he knew it was time to cut ties from his father and move on with his life. He got a job as a security guard for a local politician. The training for this job suited him and he became very adept at handling a gun. As the years rolled by, he did security jobs for more prominent politicians until fifteen years later. Here he was working for Senator Clayton Chraft. And now it seemed like he was also on a wild goose chase for some boat on the side of a mountain that no one in the past four millennia had ever set eyes on. He wanted to mourn his cousin, and here he was in a restaurant in Ankara, Turkey, waiting on some food.

Senator Chraft, you son of a—.

"Gentlemen, your breakfast is served," the waiter said as he put their meals in front of them. "Is there anything else I can get for you?" he asked, smiling at them.

"No, thank you," Hasan shot back.

In his heart, he knew Abu was right about him and his cousin, but that didn't make things any easier. The men ate their meals in silence except for the occasional off-hand remark about one thing or another. It was an uneasy morning.

CHAPTER 25

The distinguished gentlemen that made up Swanson's inner circle began to file into the boardroom of the American Civil Liberties Union offices in Washington D.C. Besides Monty Swanson, there was also Jim Quigley. Other members included the man from the state of Vermont, Jim Donohue; and from the state of Rhode Island, Bill Cunningham; and from the state of Oregon, Ted Jackson. The final two senators were from Washington state and California. They were Anita Cruise and Steve Ashley respectively. Last, but not least, was the chairman of the ACLU's Washington D.C. chapter, Elizabeth Coleman; her friends called her Lizzie. They each took their respective seats at this meeting, and Monty brought them to order. Monty already had the laptop computer setup on the table, which was also connected to a projector. That in turn was pointed at a white screen hanging from the ceiling. Monty just had to flip a switch for the screen to move silently down.

"Ladies and gentlemen, let me first start off with a bit of good news. The contacts that Chraft had waiting for his boys in Ankara, Turkey, disappeared overnight. It seems their bodies were found in the Bayindir Baraji.

That's a lake about thirty minutes east of the city. So those boys are one less thing for us to worry about." Swanson gave this news with a smile on his face, and as he did so, a look of approval appeared on each face in the room.

"Now, I'm going to show you some pictures of something I'm sure you'll all find real interesting. Lady and gentlemen, if you'll all direct your attention to the screen," Monty said, removing the piece of paper that he used for a blind on the projector screen until he was ready to show these pictures. A look of amazement crept over their faces as they all stared at the collection of photos Swanson's man had sent him just before Chraft sent his men to Turkey. There, on the screen, were actual photos from both past and present expeditions and military flyovers of Mount Ararat and something the Central Intelligence Agency had been calling the "Ararat anomaly" for over sixty years.

"Is that what it looks like?" Jim Donohue said, rising to his feet and putting his glasses on to make sure his vision was clear enough to digest what he thought he was seeing.

"What do you think it looks like?" Swanson replied, answering Donohue's question with one of his own.

"It looks like Noah's ark!" Donohue exclaimed in a curious manner. He could not believe what he was seeing.

"How do you know what the ark looks like, Jim? Have you ever seen it with your own eyes?" Swanson shot back.

"Does this mean that the photo has not been

authenticated?" Donohue asked Swanson, who was now looking at his colleague with skepticism.

"People, I know this is very heady stuff. This photo was taken by a military photographer on board a C-130 aircraft, which was a cargo plane back in the 1940s. They were returning back to England and they flew over Mount Ararat when the guy taking the pictures snapped this one." Swanson pressed the "page down" button on his laptop, producing a drawing of the ark.

A stunned look came over each of their faces.

"This is a drawing of the ark as it was described to that photographer by a man named George Hagopian. He was a boy who was raised in the foothills of Ararat. Apparently, the previous four summers from 1904 to 1908 were very hot and humid. This boy's daddy would take him up the mountain to play on the ark. This drawing is how Hagopian described it when he was old man. He died in 1972 when he was seventy-four."

Swanson finished his speech and continued to show more drawings and photos of Mount Ararat and the ark. When the slideshow ended, Lizzie Coleman asked the question that was on still on everyone's mind. "So, was that first photo authenticated and how do we know for sure what we are even looking at?"

Swanson walked to the side of the room and flipped the switch and returned the screen back to its hiding place in the ceiling. He also turned the room lights back on. After turning off his laptop, he never said a word as he walked up to the podium, and as he turned back to his small audience, his facial features turned deadly serious.

"Now, let me tell each and every one of you something, and hear me well. One of Chraft's contacts there in Ankara just happened to be a cousin to one of his boys. Now, unless I missed something, right now they're sitting in a restaurant wondering what else they're supposed to do. I have sent my nephew and another of my boys over there to make sure Ian and his guys either don't get up that mountain or don't make it back down. I personally don't care which one of these happens first. You have seen the evidence that the ark is up there. But, let me tell you what: if they do make it up that mountain and take their pictures, make their little documentary, and do whatever it is they're going to do and bring back the evidence, ladies and gentlemen, we'll be ruined.

"Right now, and for the past three decades, we have more or less controlled public thinking about the Bible, God, and religion. A woman I still look up to is Madelyn Murray O'Hare. Now, I realize that some of you may not know who this woman was, but she was the one who got prayer banned in public schools back in 1963. That came about as she was one of the litigants in the case of *Murray vs. Curlett.* That decision led the United States Supreme Court to get rid of organized prayer. Now, we can successfully sue any state, county, or local government and make them remove anything that looks like a Christian symbol. We've already sued several public schools and counties for publicly displaying those sorts of things. And we have sued them all very successfully. One case in point, we've sued a Florida county school because, in our humble opinion, the officials were using their governmental positions to promote their personal religious beliefs. And also because the school would also sponsor religious ceremonies and hold official school events at local area churches. We even successfully sued a sitting conservative who was a former chief justice of the supreme court of the state of Alabama. You can't even mention the name of God in the public forum anymore, and that is exactly what we, the American Civil Liberties Union, want. So this is the point I'm trying to make; if any of this gets out, if these boys are successful in bringing back any proof that Noah's ark does indeed exist, then we'll have a lot of people out there who call themselves Christians who will start growing something that looks a lot like a spine. After that, they'll start demanding their right to pray in public over food, for each other, and anyway else they choose to pray. Now, lady and gentlemen, I don't know about you, but I like things the way they are—being able to harass state and local governments over this God thing and have them give in to our way of thinking without so much as a word to the contrary. We cannot allow Chraft's boys to be successful in any way, shape, or form." Swanson finished his speech, one in which he was very animated.

"So what if they are successful in bringing back their documentation? What if we are unable to stop them?" Senator Ashley from California asked.

"Well, Steve, let's just say that as far as I am concerned, they won't be," Swanson said, answering the question in a matter of fact tone of voice.

"Why don't we just have them taken care of now? Who can stop us?" Ted Jackson from Oregon demanded.

"Jim, you could just call your contacts, and next thing we know, we're hearing about Chraft's boys floating facedown in the lake," Senator Jackson said, addressing his senatorial colleague.

"Ted, buddy, it's not that simple. Now, my contacts took care of some business, and those were local boys. Ian, Hasan and Abu are all Americans In this case, if we got rid of one, we'd have to get rid of all of them, and if it's all the same to you, I'd rather not have an international incident on my hands," Swanson answered with a coy smile on his face.

"That's baloney, Swanson, and you know it!" Ted Jackson retorted. Being the aggressive politician he was, to him, Chraft's boys were merely speed bumps. "You pay your contacts a little more money, and I'm sure they could find a way to get rid of Ian and the other two and no one else would know the difference," Jackson added.

"So you don't think any of their families would petition the government to find out what happened to them?" Monty asked in return. More than a little friction was starting to build between the two men.

"I still say you should make some phone calls and have Chraft's men gotten rid of immediately. That would guarantee our success at having them never come back—with or without evidence."

"See, now that's exactly why I was put in charge of this thing. We needed someone with a more level head to make these kinds of decisions," Monty finished.

Ted put his finger in Monty's face and said, "You son of a—"

"Gentlemen, gentlemen, I am sure we can continue to discuss this issue like the adults that we are," James Quigley spoke up, addressing his two colleagues. He had arrived late and slipped into the boardroom while the rest of them were looking at the slide show. The board members turned around to look at him while he casually walked up to Ted and Jim. For his age, he still walked like a very dignified man. He put his hands on Ted's shoulder.

"Ted, while I appreciate your enthusiasm for ensuring the failure of Chraft's men to come back, we must also use a more common-sense approach and be more level headed than that. Jim here has the more subtle way of making sure they don't come back, if you get my point," he said, leaning farther toward him as he finished talking.

"I get your point, James. But like the rest of you, I don't want any more evidence of that ark coming back."

"Of course you don't, Ted. And neither do we. Now that we have all seen the photos and drawings, I think we can adjourn ourselves for the night. Jim, you keep doing what you're doing. Ted, I think we can all count on your continued support," Senator Quigley said to him as he finished talking. Ted nodded in agreement as he and Jim shook hands.

"Excellent!" James continued. "Now, let's get out of here, go home, and get a good night's rest."

The board members agreed to do just that, and they began to leave the room.

Monty began to disconnect his laptop from the projector. Lizzie walked up to him while he was doing this.

"So, what's your plan for tomorrow?" she asked.

"Right now, those boys are dead in the water. Chraft is so busy trying to find out who killed his contacts, he'll be up all night making phone calls to the local police department. I wouldn't look for anything from him or his boys for at least a few days. That'll give me some time to go over a few things I have in my head," Swanson answered.

"So, we're not going to have them taken care of?" She asked him again, wanting to be sure within herself of what Monty was going to do.

"I didn't say that Lizzie. As I said before, this thing has to be handled delicately. The last thing we need is for two American boys to come up missing in Turkey. I've got some more ideas; just give me more time so that I can work my plan." He answered her, gathering his equipment up. The briefing had gone quite well, despite Ted's outburst. Now, it was time to go home. He needed his sleep for the kind of day he was going to have tomorrow.

Chapter 26

"We are going to my cousin's house. I must pay my respects. Besides, instead of waiting for a phone call, we will also have a place to sleep tonight. It seems to me that Clayton Chraft has been thrown a curveball, and he swung and missed. Now, he has to regroup, but we cannot wait that long," Hasan said as he got up from the corner table they were sitting at. They then made their way out of the restaurant. He hailed a taxi and gave the driver directions to his cousin's address, and off they sped. Although the address was across town, it was only twenty minutes away. He knew not to call Chraft, whom he also knew would be very busy making phone calls. The driver pulled up to the address Hasan had given him. He flipped the driver the required payment, and the three of them walked inside the house. His aunts, uncles, and other cousins were very glad to see him.

Chapter 27

Tyler awoke to the flight attendant's instructions of bringing his seat to the upright position. He sleepily complied and removed his earphones in the process. After a good yawn and stretch, he looked at his partner, who himself was also waking up.

"Long flight, huh, pal?" Tyler said to Mahmood, who was nodding in agreement as he too stretched and yawned. "Still mad about … things?" he asked.

Mahmood replied that he was not and that he just needed time to get his head back in the game. The plane touched down and taxied to its inbound gate. Both of them made their way to baggage claim, recovered their stuff, and then left the area to go outside the airport. A taxi took them to the hotel Uncle Monty had booked for them. After checking in, they made their way to their respective rooms and began to get settled in. After taking a shower to freshen up, Tyler picked up his cell phone and scrolled down the screen until his uncle's name was highlighted. He pushed the call button.

"Tyler, I presume you and Mahmood have gotten checked in at the hotel," Swanson said to Tyler, answering the phone.

"Yeah, we're here, Uncle Monty. I'm calling from the balcony outside my room, and the city is so well lit. It's beautiful."

"I'm sure it is, Tyler."

"Any word on Chraft's guys, Uncle Monty?"

"Well, let's just say that they're holed up in another hotel waiting for Chraft to call and let them know what they're next move should be. I swear, Chraft's got three PhD's, one of whom is a security expert working for him and right about now those boys don't know their butts from a hole in the ground. You'd think he could find boys smarter than that," Monty said, swirling his drink in his hand.

Right now, the senate was in recess for the month of August, and Monty would not have to go back to work until the day after Labor Day. Monty had a full day in the senate. He had teamed up with his senatorial colleague from Massachusetts to again attempt to erase the phrase "under God" from the Pledge of Allegiance. Never mind that here in Washington, reliefs of both Moses and the Ten Commandments were either on the front door or hung out just above it on every federal building in the District of Columbia. But for the most part, the voting public either didn't seem to realize this or didn't care.

"So, what are your plans for tomorrow?" Tyler asked his uncle.

"Get some sleep tonight. Tomorrow, I'll call you when I have more information. It seems one of my esteemed colleagues believes you need to take care of business right away but I told him I didn't see it that way. Besides, with some people showing up floating facedown in the lake just east of where you're at right now, we sure don't need an international incident on our hands. These things take both timing and coordination. But I'll continue to handle that. Just sit tight and relax for now. I'll call you tomorrow. By the way, how's Mahmood acting?"

"He's fine, Uncle Monty, just fine. We had a little talk just as we landed. Let's just say it's a good thing we have him on our side."

"Perfect, that's what I like to hear. He always was a good man for me. I have nothing but confidence in him."

"Just as you should,Uncle. Listen, let me get off here so we can go and get something to eat. I'll look forward to hearing from you tomorrow," Tyler said before he hung up the phone.

He went to get Mahmood and go to dinner.

Chapter 28

Hasan walked over to this cousin's mother and gave her a kiss on the cheek and a big hug. She told him how good it was to see him and that it had been a long time. He told her he was very sorry for her loss and that he was very fond of his cousin. She told Hasan that her son spoke of him often. Hasan then introduced Ian and Abu. Aunt Beria received them in the Turkish tradition with a kiss on the cheek and told them to make themselves comfortable. Ian and Abu also met Hasan's other cousins, aunts, and uncles who were also present in the house.

The conversation was a mix of both sorrow and joy as although one cousin was lost, another was found. After dinner, they enjoyed a few glasses of red wine. Ian was enjoying a conversation with one of Hasan's uncles, while Abu was discussing Egyptian dinner recipes with Aunt Beria's sister. One of his cousins got everyone else's attention and suggested a toast to their slain cousin, Berk.

Berk was described as a solid and strong young man of character who could be counted on for anything and was very trustworthy. They raised their glasses and drank the wine Berk's memory. Afterwards, everyone hugged each other, and both Abu and Ian expressed their condolences for the family's loss.

"Hasan, we are so very glad you came back for a visit, and again, you're friends are also welcome. I must ask, how long do you plan on staying?" Aunt Beria asked him.

"Long enough to climb Mount Ararat, find and document Noah's ark, and return to America and bring back the proof of its existence to the senator I work for," he answered her. The look on each of their faces was incredulous. Most of them, having heard of the ark, did not believe in its existence. But here was one of their own telling them what his plans were while Turkey.

"Do you believe it even exists?" she asked him.

"Personally, I am not sure, but my boss most surely does. So much in fact that he is willing to spend his entire family inheritance in proving so, and besides, he is also paying me more than enough money for my time and effort," he added, gesturing to his friends.

"I see. How are you going to get there from here? It is a long journey.'"

"I was thinking we could rent a car."

"Rent a car? For a journey that far? You'll run out of money before you get halfway. Is this American senator going to pay for this?" one of Hasan's uncles asked him.

"I am waiting for his phone call at present. He is trying to find out who killed my cousin. He paid Berk and a friend to come to the airport to pick us up. When they did not show up, I called him to find out what happened. He said he would make some phone calls to find out. I am still waiting for him to call," He informed his uncle. By now, all of his relatives were talking amongst themselves about this.

"Who is this American senator?" Hasan's uncle asked him.

"I can't say, and I really should not have brought him up to you anyway. The less people know about him or why we're here the better." Hasan said, answering his uncle. He now felt that he should have kept his big mouth shut.

"How much is the senator paying you?" Aunt Beria asked.

He took a deep breath before answering.

"He is paying me five million American dollars," Hasan said, not sure he should divulge that information. A gasp spread over his family. Although they were not sure exactly how much money that was, it sure sounded like a lot.

"Has he paid you anything so far?" his uncle asked.

"He has paid us all half now, the other half when we come back with proof the ark exists," he told them in a matter of fact tone of voice.

"How much time do you have to do this?" another cousin, whose name was Tug, asked.

"As soon as possible; however, there are other people who do not wish for our success. They are chasing us, but we don't know how far behind us they are. They could by flying here now or are already here. We don't know as of yet. If they find us, they will kill us; it's that serious. But we must leave as soon as we can, but we must find someone who knows where the ark is on Mount Ararat and how to get to it. Someone who has already been there before," Hasan answered him. He was starting to sound desperate. Ian and Abu were already feeling that way.

"I know someone who does know about this. He has actually been to the ark before. I remember him telling us bedtime stories about it when we were young."

Aunt Beria turned to face her young cousin. "Who? Who of us knows about the ark and how to get there?" she asked in absolute amazement.

"Great-grandfather Ibrahim," he answered.

Great-grandfather Ibrahim was the patriarch of the family and Aunt Beria's own father's grandfather.

"I don't remember those bedtime stories," she said to him.

"He would tell me those stories when I could not sleep. He would also tell my father those stories when he was young. Father and I would occasionally discuss this to see if either one of us believed it. He wasn't sure, and I never really did. We can go over to his house tomorrow. I have to check on him anyway. We could ask him about it then," Tug said to her. Aunt Beria nodded her head and hugged her young cousin.

CHAPTER 29

Tyler awoke early the next morning. His head was a little groggy from the ouzo he and Mahmood had after dinner the night before. The bartender had asked Tyler if he would like to try the lion's milk. Curious, Tyler admitted he would like to try that particular concoction and see how it might taste. He remembered that Mahmood had warned him to only try one and then either ask for the wine list or switch to beer. He also remembered telling Mahmood that because they were in Turkey, and might not get that chance again, he, Tyler, was going to experiment. Mahmood then simply raised his hands, palms up toward Tyler in a gesture that said, *you're on your own.*

The bartender brought Tyler his drink, and then poured some water into it, causing the liquid to turn milky-white in color. Tyler asked what the name of this drink was again, and he was reminded of its title. He lifted the drink to his nose and sniffed it. The liquor smelled like grapes to him, and he promptly raised his glass to Mahmood, who simply rolled his eyes as if to say, *let's get this over with,* and then Tyler turned it upside down and drained the fluid in one swallow.

It took his breath away, but now he was even more

intrigued. Tyler asked Mahmood if he had ever tried this drink before. Mahmood told him that he had grown up on it but was not in the mood for liquor; rather, he was more in favor of nursing his beer. Tyler promptly ordered another round for him and another beer for Mahmood, who informed his partying friend that he may want to pace himself. Tyler would hear none of the free advice Mahmood was serving and told the bartender to keep them coming. Mahmood, knowing how the night was going to end, continued to drink slowly. After Tyler's fifth round, Mahmood noticed his friend could barely talk. He told Tyler that enough was enough and that it was time to call it a night. Tyler insisted he could go another round, but Mahmood paid their tabs and started walking them back to their rooms. Inside his room, Tyler started to guard his stomach, and Mahmood escorted Tyler to the bathroom where he promptly began throwing up. After fifteen solid minutes of Tyler losing his liquor, Mahmood was finally able to walk Tyler over to his bed and dump him on it. Tyler was now fully unconscious.

"I told you to pace yourself, you old goat. Now look at you. Mid-forties and trying to drink like you're in your twenties again. I'll see you in the morning," Mahmood said shaking his head and knowing his words fell upon deaf ears. He exited the room and went to his. He got undressed and went to bed. Before he went to sleep, he lay there wondering how tomorrow was going to go. Would they run into Dr. James and the rest of them? And if they did, how would they make their deaths look like an accident? He knew how to handle a gun, but he also knew that killing them silently would be the best option. So many things to think about and so little time to get things done. Should they allow Ian and friends to get to the mountain, or take them somewhere and kill them silently? Mahmood knew he needed rest. He leaned over and turned off the lamp beside his bed and drifted off into a fitful sleep.

"Good morning, oh one who thought he could drink the lion's milk and survive," He said, greeting Tyler the next morning and waving a cup of coffee under Tyler's nose. Tyler pulled himself upright in bed and took the coffee from Mahmood.

"How many did I have last night?" he asked, rubbing his eyes and face.

"Five," Mahmood informed him.

"Man, I don't remember a thing past two," Tyler responded and began to sip the hot liquid from its cup.

"My head is pounding. Why didn't you stop me?"

"Do you not remember me telling you to pace yourself?"

Tyler thought for a moment and did indeed remember that part of the evening.

"No more lion's milk for me," he said, getting out of bed and walking to the bathroom.

"Has your uncle called yet?" Mahmood asked.

"I don't know. I haven't checked my messages yet. Call the voicemail and see," Tyler said from behind a closed bathroom door.

Mahmood heard water flow from the showerhead as he began checking messages.

There were two from Tyler's mom—one from her leaving a message and another one asking why he had not returned her call. She was also asking what Turkey was like as she and his father were coming up on some vacation time and wanted to know if it looked as nice a place to visit as it did on one of the many vacation websites she had been looking at. There was another one from a male friend who was inviting Tyler over to dinner, and in the background Mahmood could hear the man's wife telling her husband to ask Tyler when he was going to get married. The last message was from Uncle Swanson.

"Tyler, call me when you get this. I think I may have some unpleasant news."

Mahmood put the phone down and sat in the chair opposite the bed. He turned the radio on that was on the shelf, and out flowed music by someone named Zeynep Dizdar. Mahmood had heard of her before and liked her music. To him, it sounded a little on the techno side but also a more modern traditional sound in Turkish music, and he appreciated that.

As her song ended, Tyler emerged from the bathroom.

"Call your uncle; he said he may have some unpleasant news," Mahmood told him.

With his towel still wrapped around his waist, Tyler walked over to his nightstand beside his bed and picked up his cell phone and called his uncle.

"Tyler, you obviously didn't leave your phone on last night," Monty said, sounding disappointed.

"No Uncle Monty, sorry. We went out for dinner and it needed to be recharged, so I left it in the room."

"Well, what I need to tell you is we can't find Ian and those boys. Seems that after Chraft's contacts were disposed of, our boys decided to take matters into their own hands and found another place to stay. They didn't go to the hotel like they were supposed to, and now we can't find them. Why don't you see if Mahmood can work some of his magic and see where they might be? But now, here's the thing; if you can find them, trail them. Don't do anything to them yet. What I want you boys to do is just that, trail them and let them lead you to Ararat and the ark. What you're going to do is make sure they don't come back when all of you get up to the ark. I want you to kill them, and then I want you to figure out a way to make sure their bodies don't come back. Are you following me, son?"

"Perfectly Uncle Monty. We'll let them lead us to the ark and then Mahmood will do what he does, no sweat."

"Okay, now I'm counting on you boys to get this done. There'll be a lot of people who are going to appreciate your services after this is all over, and I'll be one of them. You do this, and there might be a little something extra in it for you. So are we clear in what you're supposed to do?"

"Absolutely Uncle Monty. Don't worry. You can count on us."

"By the way, call your mother. She thinks she and your dad might want to fly off to Turkey for a vacation.

She said she called you twice and you haven't called her back. Now what kind of a son doesn't call his mother?"

A bothersome look came over Tyler's face.

"I'll call her, Uncle Monty. Just tell her I've sort of been busy for me, okay?"

"She's your mother, son. Besides, I'm too busy taking care of things here. Just call and talk to her for a while; you'll be all right."

"Okay, Uncle Monty. I'll call her this afternoon," Tyler said as he hung up.

"I'll call her after we're done here," he said to himself.

"Now, we have to find Ian and his guys. They're not at their hotel. Is there any way you can find them, Mahmood?"

He thought for a moment.

"Let me see what I can do," he finally said.

CHAPTER 30

Aunt Beria, Hasan, Ian, and Abu, along with a few cousins knocked on Great-grandfather Ibrahim's front door, turned the knob, opened the door, and slowly announced their arrival as they walked in. The housekeeper told them to come in and have a seat as she was busy washing clothes and cleaning up after breakfast. Semiramis broke from her morning routine to speak to Aunt Beria.

"So, how is he?" she asked her. Semiramis took notice of the three strangers seated on the couch along with Aunt Beria.

"Oh, I'm sorry, Semiramis. This is Hasan and his friends, Abu and Ian. They came with us to check on Great-grandfather Ibrahim."

Semiramis nodded to the three men to acknowledge their presence.

"Would you all like some tea?" she asked them, wanting each of them to feel at home.

They collectively agreed that tea would be nice, and she went to the kitchen and brought back the tea set. Everything was already fully prepared as Ibrahim had always enjoyed tea with his breakfast. Semiramis poured each of them a cup, and they sat back on the couch to enjoy Semiramis' hospitality.

"How's he doing?" Aunt Beria asked again.

"He is well. Being old, he has good days as well as bad ones. But his mind is still sharp and his sense of humor is still intact," Semiramis answered in a rather positive tone and instantly putting them more at ease. Although they did come to check on him, now they also had questions—questions they hoped Ibrahim could answer. Semiramis had been Ibrahim's caregiver for the past twenty years.

When he was a young man, Ibrahim loved to travel. He had traveled all over Turkey and had been to Iraq and to Egypt. When he was in his thirties, he had traveled to eastern Turkey and visited a friend of his who lived there. Nima was also a young man Ibrahim met when he was living for a time in Cairo, Egypt. Ibrahim had found work in a hotel there, and Nima had already been working there for a few months. They formed an instant friendship, and as the years rolled along, Nima said it was time for him to return home to his village that lay in the foothills of Mount Ararat. Nima suggested to Ibrahim that he come along as well and that Nima had written many letters home telling his family about Ibrahim. Nima's family had written back on several occasions, telling him how much they would like to meet Ibrahim. Ibrahim had been saving money over the years and agreed to accompany Nima to his home. Nima also told Ibrahim about his sister and that she would like to meet him as well. They flew to Ankara and then it was a long bus ride to Nima's village of Lake Van. In his youth, Nima had been a shepherd boy but he wanted no part of that life. He left when he was a teenager and now that he was also in his thirties, he was homesick for the first time in his life, and he knew it was to come home.

When Nima saw his home the first time in decades, he noticed how much it had changed. The village was no longer a village, but looked more like a small city. They arrived at his parents' house and knocked on the door. His mother let him and Ibrahim in and the celebration began. Friends and family from all over the city were there to welcome the prodigal son and his friend home. The feast lasted all weekend, and Nima noticed his little sister, Salime, had taken to Ibrahim. Ibrahim was told that he could stay for as long as he wanted, and that suited him just fine seeing that he, too, was also falling for Salime. Her name in Turkish meant "good and useful," and in Ibrahim's eyes, she was the most beautiful young woman he had ever seen. She was five feet six inches tall with dark hair that went down to her waist. She also had dark eyes that seemed to peer into his soul and a face that to him was the one of a goddess. Eventually, Salime and Ibrahim married, and he fathered several children. One of whom was Aunt Beria's own grandfather, whose name was Aral.

Ibrahim met a man named George Hagopian who would tell Ibrahim stories about how his father would take him up the mountain to see Noah's ark. George had asked Ibrahim if he had ever seen the ark, and Ibrahim had to admit that he had not. George offered to take him up to see the ark when the weather turned warm that summer. Early one morning, both George and Ibrahim started up the mountain. They brought enough provisions to last them for a few days. George took Ibrahim the usual way that George knew up to the ark. George took him up Mount Ararat and past the Ahora Gorge. George explained to Ibrahim that the gorge was formed during an 1840 earthquake, which caused a massive icefall in the gorge, which dammed up for a little while. It eventually broke through and flooded the monastery and the original village of Ahora with a wall of water, ice, mud, and rocks. George pointed in the direction that the ark was. On the way, George commented on what a nice day they had in order to go and see the ark. The higher they climbed, the colder it got, but since they were climbing, their coats were sufficient enough to keep them warm. They also stopped at the grave of Saint Jacob of Nisbis and who was also the first Christian to search for Noah's Ark and had lunch. After eating they pitched a tent for the night and settled down. They woke up early the next morning and once again began to climb up the mountain. The climb grew more precipitous, and George informed friend that they were almost there. George then crested a small butte, turned back, and helped Ibrahim up and over it as well.

George looked at Ibrahim and then told him to look in the direction he was pointing. Ibrahim followed the direction his friend's finger was pointing, and there, located on a rock ledge over a cliff and partially covered by snow and ice, stood the remains of Noah's ark. George asked Ibrahim to follow him so that they could take a better look at it. They walked right up to the side of the ark. Ibrahim touched the ark and commented on how it felt like stone. George motioned again for Ibrahim to follow. They came to the end of the ark. About twelve feet up was what looked like a ladder attached to the side of it. George bent down and hoisted his friend upon his shoulders, and Ibrahim grabbed hold of the bottom two rungs and pulled himself up. He turned around and extended his hand to George and pulled him up as well. The two men climbed the ladder to the top of the ark and began to walk along its surface.

"So you used to play on this boat when you were a child. How did your father even know where it was?" Ibrahim asked George. He had some questions for his friend.

"Oral tradition, my friend. My father's father would bring him up here to play on it as well. Remember, Ibrahim, I grew up in the village in the foothills of this mountain, and my father has brought me up here many times in my youth. I brought you up here because I wanted you to see it. You see those slits in the side of the top part? Those were windows and not very big ones, as you can see."

"Can you see inside from up here?"

"Not really; although it's very bright out here, it's darker in there. Besides, as you can see, the awning over the windows really prevents any light from getting in. I have shined a flashlight down the inside, but the light is so small and the inside is still too dark to really see anything," George confessed to Ibrahim as they continued to walk along the top surface of the ark.

"How long do you suppose it took Noah to make this thing?"

"Well, judging by just the immense size of the outside of the ark and not knowing still what the inside looks like, plus the fact that his sons were also helping him, I could only guess it took him years to build this," George answered Ibrahim, gesturing as he did. George really had no idea how long it took for Noah and his help to build this thing.

Ibrahim nodded in agreement, and they began to walk back toward the end of the ship where the ladder was. After a while, George looked skyward and noticed it was getting late and that they should climb off the ark and start their descent down the mountain. They lowered themselves from the ladder and began the trek back down the mountain. While George was still somewhat giddy from being on top of the ark for the first time in years, Ibrahim was still trying to digest what he had just seen and done. The ark had come to rest on this very spot over four thousand years ago and here he and George were walking away from the ark and occasionally turning around to look at it again. He had just climbed to the top of that ark for the first time in his life, but George's father would bring him up here as a child to play on it. Other kids had a yard or a street to play on; George had an ark. They climbed back over the same butte as they had before; he turned around and took one last look at it. It was indeed a sight to behold, and Ibrahim could not take his eyes off it.

"Let's go, my friend, we have to be back down at the grave of Saint Jacob before nightfall, there, we'll camp again for the night." George said to a still stunned Ibrahim. They turned and began the long trek back down the mountain.

Chapter 31

"Tyler, tell me you got good news, son. Right about now, I sure could use some," Uncle Monty said to his nephew as Monty enjoyed the view from the rocking chair on his front porch. The senate was now in full recess until August. Monty had thirty days in which to enjoy his long vacation, which also meant he could devote more time to this current project.

"Indeed I do, Uncle Monty. Mahmood contacted the people you did for help with Chraft's contacts. Through a friend of a friend of an old acquaintance, we were able to find out where Ian, Abu, and Hasan were staying. It should have been the first place we thought of; Hasan went to his aunt's house to mourn his cousin. They live outside of the city, but we have eyes on them right now. But just so you know, they are now at Hasan's great-grandfather's house, and it looks like they're going to be there all day. If all you want Mahmood and me to do is follow them, we're going to need a few things. There are a couple of stores here in town. I'll put some things on my card and just keep you informed."

"That sounds like a plan to me, Tyler. Just keep your eyes on those boys and keep me informed. I've got a few rounds of golf to play with the boys this afternoon. If you need any more help, just let me know," Monty said before hanging up. He got up from his chair and proceeded to the car parked in his driveway. He turned the ignition, and the car roared to life. Before he pulled out of his driveway, a smile came across his face.

"Yeah, that boy's got a future," he said to himself.

He pulled out of his driveway smiling.

It was going to be a good day.

Chapter 32

Mahmood was not pleased. He could not believe his ears when he heard Tyler tell Swanson he was going to use his credit card to buy the supplies they needed for the trip to Ararat. Mahmood was going to put a stop to this right now.

"For being the nephew of a United States senator and for someone who was born wealthy and privileged as you, you're not very bright," he said to Tyler in a matter-of-fact tone of voice, putting his fingers on Tyler's chest to drive home his point. He was very angry.

"Excuse me? What do you mean I'm not very bright? And so what if I was born rich? Does that make you jealous, Mahmood?" he replied. Tyler was incredulous and amazed at him. So far, everything had gone perfectly, and now Mahmood was angry because Tyler wanted to spend money on what they needed. And as far as him being born rich, so what?

Mahmood took a deep breath and explained to Tyler why putting guns and ammunition on a credit card would be a most stupid thing.

"Do you forget why we are here? Do you forget what we are about to do? If you buy one thing here, it will create a paper trail that will lead right back to you. What if, after we kill them, their bodies are found? And do you really think your uncle will bail us out of trouble? The man has shown very little concern for anyone but himself. This is supposed to look like an accident. There are also rebels who roam that area of the mountain who don't like foreigners looking around up there. But they can be bought, and besides, the men we have watching Ian and his gang also have access to the black market. We will ask them to get us guns and ammunition. Do not spend money here, my friend. I will tell our men what we want, and they will tell us how much it will cost. And they will bring us what we need, and we will pay them at that time. You will simply take out as much cash as we will need; that way, it will only look like you're a tourist having a good time. No paper trail, no nothing. Do you understand that?" He finished speaking and walked back to the bathroom to splash water on his face. He had to calm down, and Mister Moneybags just said the wrong thing. There were many other ways to could be done, but a death on Ararat could be made to look like an accident if it were done right. Besides, people do die while climbing mountains, right? What makes this mountain so different? He walked back into the living room where Tyler was sitting on the couch. He knew Mahmood had a very good point.

"Okay, Mahmood. We'll do it your way. Call the guys, and tell them what we need and ask them how much it will cost. And you're right; we don't need a paper trail."

Mahmood picked up the cell phone and made a phone call.

Chapter 33

It was now toward evening, and Ibrahim was being led out to the living room by Semiramis. She had already prepared the evening meal and had invited her guests to stay for dinner. Ibrahim was an old man in his nineties, and he needed some help with walking as he leaned on his cane and let her lead him to the table. His eyes were weak, but his ears perked up when he heard those gathered around the table rise to their feet to honor his presence. He took his place at the head of the table and sat down. His guests then took their seats. He reached into his shirt pocket and took out his reading glasses and put them on. He was too old to drive anymore, but he could read and recognize people with his glasses on.

"God be praised!" he said aloud as he looked around the table. He saw his guests were relatives he had not seen in a while.

"Great-grandfather, so nice to see you again," Hasan said to him, taking his hand and kissing his cheek. One by one, the rest of them rose to greet Ibrahim with a kiss. Ian shook his hand and also extended his greeting. After Ibrahim said the blessing, he invited everyone to begin eating.

He was asked about his health and whether or not he was used to having someone take care of him. He told them he very much enjoyed having someone else in the house so he did not have to do the dishes. His comment brought laughter to the comfortable atmosphere at the table. As dinner progressed, Aunt Beria told stories of her memories of him when she was a little girl. The other cousins did the same, and then Hasan mentioned his family.

"Did you and your father ever come to terms?" Ibrahim asked.

Hasan was stunned. *How did he know?*

Ibrahim read the look on Hasan's face and told him he knew everything.

"Yes, we did, right before he died," Hasan managed to answer.

"That is good. And how is your mother?" Ibrahim asked.

"She is well, Ibrahim. She wants me to come home to visit, and it has been a while since I have seen her."

"I would suggest you do that soon—one can never know when God sees fit to bring one of his children home. Speaking of visits, what brings Hasan and his friends for a visit?"

Everyone looked at Hasan, who looked nervous as he prepared to ask the burning question they all had on their minds. He cleared his throat before he spoke.

"Ibrahim, there is a question I must ask you. It is the reason for my, Ian, and Abu's visit. I work for a United States senator who has a deep interest, one might even call it a passion, but it's of something of a biblical nature. This senator, he believes that Noah's ark exists, and he has sent us here to go up the mountain to photograph and document the ark. We were told that you know more about this and that we should come to you. We were told by Adem that you know about the ark, and how to get up to it. Is this true, Ibrahim?"

Even though Hasan had regretted admitting this to Aunt Beria and his uncle, he now thought it no longer mattered as they needed to get to the mountain and they really had no way to get there. But from what they've been told, Ibrahim knew about the ark.

A smile came across Ibrahim's face as he looked at one of the youngest cousins in the family.

"Ah, so you remember the bedtime stories I used to tell you as a child. That is good. I have told these stories from generation to generation," Ibrahim replied.

"Is the ark up there, Ibrahim?" Aunt Beria asked. Now her curiosity was piqued. Ibrahim did know about the ark.

"I was a young man when I first set my eyes upon the ark. My friend George took me up there once and I would make the trek myself when I could and the weather permitted. I have taken several people up the mountain to the ark in those days. But there were also times we would get almost to the ark and the weather would force us back down the mountain, or the local rebels would point their guns at us and take all of our possessions and then force us to turn back."

"Why was that, Ibrahim?" Hasan asked.

"Hasan, the mountain is on the border with Iran and Armenia. Because of this, the rebels are able to trade weapons and ammunition or whatever else they need. The black market flourishes in that region. One can lose his life on Ararat, and no one else would know. It is a very dangerous place. But to answer your question, Beria; yes, the ark does exist."

Everyone had stopped eating as they became mesmerized with the story of his experience of Noah's ark.

"Let me tell you of the stories I have heard concerning the ark. In 1973, there was a man, an American astronaut, who led an expedition up the mountain. His name was James Irwin. They did not find it at the time. But many, many years before, another man did. His name was Haji Yearam. His father took him up the mountain in 1856. He mentioned that it had been an unusually hot summer and that the snow and glaciers had melted more than usual. At that time, however, there were no rebels, and the Armenians were afraid to take anyone up there as they feared God's wrath. Haji's father also took some other men along. They wanted to prove that the ark did not exist. They found the ark and went inside it, as there was a doorway they went through. The door itself was missing. The doorway was immense in its size. These men were atheists and flew into a rage that they were now standing inside an ark that they did not want to believe exists. These men, all three of them, took a solemn vow that none of them would speak of this again. Haji died in 1915; he was seventy-five years old. Three years later and on his deathbed, one of the atheists told his story of finding the ark. Also, just before the outbreak of World War II, the Russian Czar Nicholas had heard about the sighting of the ark on the mountain. The Russian soldiers found what the Turkish soldiers did in 1840 after the earthquake that formed the Ahora Gorge. Stories were printed in newspapers at that time but no one believed them. The Russian soldiers found the ark and went inside it and also took photographs and measurements. Sadly, however, the courier that the soldiers sent back to the czar with that information was captured before he could reach Nicholas. The Bolshevik Revolution had begun, and the courier's material had been taken away and was never found again."

The family could not believe their ears. Ibrahim did indeed know much about the ark. His mind was as sharp as ever even though he was an old man.

"There have been far too many sightings of Noah's ark to talk about. But, Hasan, how are you going to get there?" Ibrahim asked his great-great nephew.

"That is why we came to you, Ibrahim. You know much about the ark as you have been there. Can you get us there?"

Ibrahim leaned forward and put his hand on Hasan's.

"Hasan, if you really want to get there, I will show you how, but I warn you: all of you really have to want this and want it bad. It is a very dangerous thing to go looking for the ark. As I mentioned before, there was a time when one could climb the mountain and see it. Now, there are people besides this senator you speak of who does not want you to go up there who will kill you if they see or find you. Climbing the mountain to find the ark is not for the faint of heart. Although it is an extinct volcano that does not mean it is not still prone to earthquakes."

Ian, Abu, and Hasan looked at each other without speaking. They had already come this far. They could not turn back. Besides, from what Ibrahim just told them, the ark did exist and there was a way up to it. There had also been multiple sightings of the ark by a lot of people over the years.

By now, it was late in the evening, and Ibrahim was growing tired. He grabbed his cane and stood to his feet. He looked at Hasan, Ian, and Abu and said, "Stay a few more days. My house is yours. I know a man who can gather the things you will need for your journey. I will talk to him and tell him what you have told me." Ibrahim turned to leave the table, and as he did, the rest of them rose to their feet. After Ibrahim was put to bed, Semiramis returned to clear the table and put the dishes in the sink. *I'll do them tomorrow,* she thought to herself as she wiped the countertop and the table down one last time.

She gave each of them a blanket. Abu took the couch, Hasan took the recliner, and Ian wound up on the floor. Semiramis came back with a pillow for each one. As they lay there winding down from dinner and the stories Ibrahim had just told them, they wondered what might lie ahead. Who did he know that could get them up there? What sort of provisions would they need? Would they run into rebels or experience an earthquake? They had many questions with no answers at this time. But now they also started to realize that they were one step closer to getting to Ararat than they were yesterday, and tomorrow was another day.

CHAPTER 34

Hasan was up early. He needed to talk to Chraft. It had already been almost a week, and no phone call. He could rest assured that Swanson's boys were definitely keeping in touch with him.

"Hasan, how are things? I have been trying for a couple of days now to find out who killed your cousin—"

"Forget about it," Hasan interrupted. "We have a way to Ararat and to find the ark."

"How so?" Clayton asked.

"My great-grandfather Ibrahim. He's been to the ark when he was a young man; he's told us stories of others who also tried to find the ark. Some were successful; some were not. But he is going to make a call to someone who can get us up there."

"Excellent! What is his price?"

"Somehow, I don't think there is one. When he was talking to us about it, he was very animated and still excited about it after all these years. We'll have to wait, however, until all the details are in place. That's going to take a couple of more days. I'll get back to you on that."

"Sounds good to me. And, Hasan, my sympathies

and condolences to you and your family. They're in my thoughts and prayers."

"Thank you. I'll call when plans are finalized," Hasan said and then hung up the phone. He went back inside the house where everyone was sitting down to breakfast. Hasan took a seat and extended morning greetings to all. Ibrahim looked especially cheerful this morning.

"I will call an old friend of mine today and see if he is able to get you to Ararat. He had to stop leading expeditions up there due to poor health. But he knows people who can get you to and up the mountain. And remember, the ark has been up there for over four thousand years and its not going anywhere anytime soon," Ibrahim said to each of them.

"True, but let's also hope Swanson's boys don't think the opposite and try to crash our party," Ian said before sipping his coffee.

"You mentioned that others were chasing you. Who are these people?" Ibrahim asked. The only other time he knew of someone being in danger with any kind of ark documentation was the courier of the Russian platoon that went up there right before the beginning of the Bolshevik Revolution.

"Ibrahim, what Hasan didn't mention last night was that there is another senator named Swanson. He has men working for him who are after us. Swanson does not want the ark to be found. And he doesn't want it to be found bad enough for him and some of his other guys to have paid us a visit to our hotel rooms the night before we left the States to fly here. He was pretty adamant about it. But he never told us why he did not want the ark to be found. When he and his guys left, we were smuggled out of the hotel by Chraft's guys. There is something on that mountain, Ibrahim, that's got some people upset. But it's also got some people mighty curious. But the bottom line for us is that we have already been paid half of his offer to go up Ararat. We can't back out now," Ian explained to him.

"You're doing this for money?" Ibrahim asked.

"At first yes. But in talking to Chraft before this whole thing even started and again in being visited by Swanson and also in talking to you, we want to go up there and see if it is, in fact, really there. If it is, we will do what we came here to do—document the ark. I've got to tell you, Ibrahim, for two United States senators to be fighting over this behind the scenes, then something is going on up that mountain," Ian finished, and at the rest of his breakfast.

When everyone was done, Semiramis cleaned the table and the rest of the family retired to the living room.

"Ian, this senator who doesn't want the ark to be documented, even though he didn't tell you why, what is your impression of him?" Ibrahim asked, relaxing on the couch.

"Not a good one. For some reason, he does not want any evidence of the ark brought back to America. So much so that he is willing to have us killed for it, and that's all we know," Ian said, motioning to Abu and Hasan.

A curious look came over Ibrahim's face.

Chapter 35

"We will need four guns and lots of ammunition and also binoculars and enough provisions to last a week on the mountain. We will also need a guide, someone who knows the area backward and forward. How much money will the arms dealers want to leave us alone?" Mahmood asked his contacts to the black market. They needed to gather supplies soon, and they did not want to have to wait.

"Five thousand for your supplies, and I will get back to you on the other thing. Give me one day to work on this. I will call you at this time tomorrow," Mahmood's contact told him.

With that, he hung up the phone and relayed the information to Tyler, who was enjoying a drink on the balcony overlooking the city. Tyler agreed to the monetary necessities of the provisions and the twenty-four hours on the phone call. Tyler invited Mahmood to join. He sat down on the chair beside Tyler and enjoyed the sounds of the city below.

CHAPTER 36

Ibrahim got on the phone and pushed some buttons. On the other end of the line, his old friend picked up. They exchanged pleasantries, and Ibrahim told his friend he was sorry that he had not called recently. Ibrahim said that he had some new acquaintances that wanted to go up Mount Ararat and document Noah's ark and that they needed provisions for one week. Tents, sleeping bags, a few horses or mules to carry it all, and a digital camera and recorder for documentation purposes. Ibrahim's friend asked for a day to get everything together. Ibrahim was also told what the fee would be and that he already had a guide up the mountain in mind. They reminisced for a short time about their trips up Ararat, and they wished each other well before hanging up the phone.

"I have great news; my friend has a guide for you already. But he will need one day to get everything else in order. You will also need 5,923 lira to fund your expedition," Ibrahim informed them.

"That's no problem, one of us will go to the bank today and have that amount wired over," Abu said.

"But won't that cause a paper trail?" he added.

"We have to pay for this someway, but we can't

involve Chraft. We will simply tell him he owes one of us some money. I'm sure he won't mind paying one of us back. Remember, we're tourists and all we're doing is climbing the mountain and having a good time," Hasan replied. He didn't think they would have to pay for the expedition due to Ibrahim's connections, but he also wanted to get things in motion as soon as possible and those connections required a fee; so be it. With the five million dollar fee Chraft was paying them, what's a few more dollars anyway?

Hasan and Aunt Beria went to the bank and returned an hour later with the required amount wrapped in an envelope. Hasan handed it over to Ibrahim.

"We will also need a global positioning system and a satellite phone," he informed Ibrahim as Ibrahim picked up the phone to dial his friend's number.

"Not to worry; yours is not the first expedition she has led up Ararat," Ibrahim told him.

"She?" Abu commented.

Almost speechless, Ibrahim punched the numbers and rolled his eyes.

Chapter 37

"They went to the bank and walked out with what looked like an envelope full of money. Then they went back to the house. It seems they are mounting their own expedition to the mountain. What do want us to do?" Mahmood's men asked, ready to kill all three of Chraft's men on the spot.

"Do nothing, but continue to watch. Let us know the moment they leave. How are things coming with our request?" Mahmood asked, eager to get this cat-and-mouse game rolling further and onto its climax at the top of Mount Ararat.

"You will need six thousand lira. As soon as you deliver the money, I can have everything you need in twenty-four hours," the contact informed Mahmood.

"What are Chraft's guys doing right now?"

"Still sitting inside the house. There is not a lot of activity from where we are sitting."

"Meet me down the street. There is a small diner there. You will come inside, and we will give you the money there."

"Won't that be a little obvious?"

"Don't worry, it will be very inconspicuous."

Mahmood's contact hung up the phone and preceded

to the diner he instructed him to go to. Thirty minutes later, his contacts walked into the small diner, and he waved them over to the table he and Tyler were sitting at.

"Gentlemen, we will do this very informally as we do not want our names to be known."

Both Tyler and Mahmood agreed to this part of the business transaction.

"Do you have the money?" the contact asked.

Mahmood nodded that he did.

"I'm handing you a magazine under the table; take it."

He did as he was instructed.

"Put the money inside the magazine, put it on the table, and then slide it back over to me."

Again, Mahmood did as he was instructed. His contact took the magazine back and opened the first page. He opened the envelope to count the money. When he was satisfied, he closed the envelope and then the magazine.

"I will call you this time tomorrow. Everything will be ready—transportation and food. You will get your guns and ammunition when you arrive at your destination. Everything will be okay," the contact said, leaning in toward both Mahmood and Tyler as he finished his talk. Tyler felt at a loss on how to deal with this situation. He looked at Mahmood, who was dealing with it just fine.

"We will leave now. I will call you tomorrow."

The contact nodded to both Tyler and Mahmood, and then he and his partner got up to leave.

"They didn't look like they belonged to the black

market," Tyler remarked as he watched them walk out the door.

"What is someone associated with the black market supposed to look like?" Mahmood asked Tyler in return.

"I don't know. I guess I had some preconceived notion that they would look more like criminals."

"And what does a criminal look like?"

Tyler had no answer for this as he was beginning to get Mahmood's point.

"Tyler, the black market is a business just like any other. The way to conduct business may not be legal but is still a business just the same," he said to Tyler, growing a bit perturbed at him. Mahmood sighed and shook his head.

It must be that wealthy upbringing and Harvard education. One would think with that kind of education Tyler would be smarter than that, he thought to himself.

"Let's go. We need to go back to the hotel room and wait for a phone call," Mahmood said, and they got up from the table and made their way to the front door.

It sure is busy here in Ankara, Tyler thought to himself as he looked around and then climbed back into the car. The meeting with Mahmood's contacts made him feel a little uneasy, but Mahmood took it all in stride. He thought about asking Mahmood how he knew about the black market but thought better of it. The more important thing now was that everything was beginning to move forward and Mahmood was making it all happen. The two of them were silent on the drive back to their hotel room.

CHAPTER 38

Tyler's cell phone went off, rousing him from sleep. He looked at the screen; it was Uncle Monty.

"Hello, Uncle Monty."

"Morning, Tyler. How's my favorite nephew?"

"Still sleeping until you called. What's up?"

"Well, I was about to ask you the same thing. Any news I should know about?"

Tyler sat up right in bed.

"We now have a contact here that is going to provide us with transportation to the mountain, among other things that we need to say goodbye to Chraft's guys. Mahmood knew some business people here who could do that for us. They should be calling us back this afternoon."

"Mahmood knew some business people—I like how you put that. How much do these people charge for business transactions?"

"Six thousand lira and that includes all the trimmings. Mahmood knows how to make things happened here, Uncle Monty."

"He sure does; he's one of them. You'll learn a lot from him, Tyler."

Mahmood knocked on Tyler's door. He got up to let him in.

"Well, I got to go. It's a nice day, and there's good fishing out on the lake today. Sounds like you boys got things well in hand. Keep me posted, Tyler, and tell Mahmood good job for me, would you?"

"Of course, Uncle Monty, will do." He hung up his cell phone as Mahmood brought Tyler a fresh cup of coffee.

"What did Swanson say?" he asked curiously.

"He said good job on finding those business people and, of course, to keep him informed."

Mahmood sipped his coffee and winked at Tyler. His phone rang again.

"Hello?"

"It's me. We have everything you need to make your trip. Your transportation is waiting for you downstairs as we speak. Everything else will be provided for as planned."

"Who is our contact there? And where exactly are we going that's at the mountain?"

"He will contact you. I have described both of you to him, and he and his team are ready for you. You will go to the city of Do ubeyazıt. It is close to Ararat and provides a base from which to attempt to climb the mountain."

"Thank you very much for your help," Tyler said as he covered the mouthpiece and told Mahmood the news. He went back to his room to grab a backpack full of clothes.

"You must also hurry; the others have already left for Ararat."

"How long ago did they leave?"

"About an hour ago. But don't panic. That gives you more than enough of a cushion to tail them. Your driver knows where he is going, so enjoy the ride."

"Got it, and thanks again." Tyler hung up the phone and hurriedly got dressed. Mahmood knocked on the door, and Tyler walked out with his own backpack full of clothes. They took the elevator down to the lobby and checked out of the hotel. They walked outside, and there was their car and driver waiting for them. Tyler and Mahmood quickly climbed into the car and the driver sped toward Ian, Abu, Hasan, and Mount Ararat.

Chapter 39

"Did Ibrahim happen to mention who our female guide is?" Abu asked Hasan, who shook his head indicating that he did not.

"Only that she has been up the mountain several times before and knows we're coming," Hasan then answered back. They were now an hour outside of the city of Ankara and on their way to Mount Ararat and possibly Noah's ark. They were now heading east on the E-88, one of the many state roads and motor ways in the country of Turkey. The E roads were a part of the European Agreement on Main International Traffic Arteries. One could travel the entire country on these roads, which were much like the European autobahns. They had just passed the town of Elmada , and the city of Kirikkale was another forty-five minutes away depending on how fast one drove. Even though the speed limit sign showed one hundred and twenty kilometers, or seventy-two miles per hour, their driver was going ninety miles per hour.

"You'd better slow down, or we might get a ticket," Ian said the driver, whose name was Asil.

Just then, another car passed them by.

"Geez, how fast was he going?" Ian asked.

"One hundred and sixty kilometers per hour," Asil replied.

"How fast is that in American?"

"One hundred miles per hour," Asil informed him.

"Dr. James, on the E roads, there are no set speed limits. Only recommended ones so please just sit back and enjoy the ride," Asil said to Ian with a smile. "I have been driving on these roads since I was sixteen. Relax," he informed Ian.

Just then another car passed them by. Ian did as he was told.

"How far to Lake Van?" Ian asked Asil.

"Twelve hundred and thirty-four kilometers, or about a fourteen-hour drive. But we still have to stop along the way. Dr. James, everything has been planned. Again, relax."

Ian laid his head against the headrest and went to sleep. In the back of the van they were in, Abu and Hasan began to munch on the roast beef sandwiches that had already been made for them. They washed the sandwiches down with cups of coffee from the thermos that came with the sandwiches as well. As they ate, they watched the countryside go by, admiring the beauty of the fields, farmland, and towns they went through. Turkey was indeed a beautiful country. Soon enough both of them stretched out on their seats and went to sleep.

Chapter 40

"How are you going to find them in this traffic?" Tyler asked Arslin.

"I know what kind of car they are driving and the license plate number," he answered Tyler.

"How do you know that?"

"I was told that information before I left to come and pick you guys up. Do they know you're following them?" Arslin asked.

"We don't think they even know we're here," Tyler replied.

"Then it's a good thing we're not far behind," he said to Tyler as he pushed a little harder down on the accelerator.

"You must understand, a lot of people go to Mount Ararat when they visit this country. A lot of pilgrims made the trek over there in the hope that they will catch a glimpse of the ark. Then there are those who just want to climb the mountain. There are few places in the Ararat region from which those expeditions can start. But we will find and follow them from a distance, and they will show us the way." Tyler nodded his head in an understanding way. Now he felt confident they would find the van

Chraft's men were in and eventually get the job done they had been sent to do. Just then, the driver motioned for Tyler to look straight ahead. Right in front of them about fifty yards away, was the van they were looking for.

"I only see the driver," Tyler said, looking at it through the binoculars that were in the bag stashed under his seat.

"The rest of them must be asleep," Arslin replied.

"I need to go to the bathroom," Mahmood said from his seat in the back of the van.

"Be patient, when they stop, we stop," Arslin replied to him

"But they will see us," Mahmood retorted.

"No, they won't. After they do what they have to do, we will pull in after they leave, do our business, and then simply catch up to them," Arslin said.

The look on Mahmood's face was one of the hopes that Chraft's men would stop soon.

CHAPTER 41

"Hey, guys, wake up. We're stopping in Yozgat for gas. You can get out here and use the bathroom and stretch if you need to," Asil said, pulling into the Shell station and up to the pump. As soon as he stopped, the three men couldn't get out of the van fast enough to get to the bathroom. They each found empty stalls and the sound of body fluids hitting the standing water could be heard simultaneously. They washed their hands and exited the bathroom. They went back outside to the van as Asil was pouring the last liter of gas into the tank.

"What city did you say this was?" Ian asked.

"This is Yozgat. Very nice, don't you think?" he asked Ian.

"Yes, it's very pretty," Ian answered back.

"Is everyone ready? I must go in and pay for the gas and use the bathroom, and then we'll be off," Asil told everyone.

"Are you holding up okay, Asil?" Hasan asked.

"I am fine, Hasan. Get in; I'll be back in a few minutes," he said walking toward the front door of the gas station.

Five minutes later, Asil came back carrying an apple pastry and a large mug of coffee. He got into the van and cranked the ignition. He pulled out of the Shell station and got back on the road.

Two minutes later, Arslin pulled into the station, and the scene replayed itself. Two men could not get out of the van fast enough. Mahmood ran past Tyler on his way to the bathroom. Arslin put the gas nozzle into the tank and started to laugh as he began to fill the van.

Ten minutes later, the two men exited the bathroom feeling much better than when they went in. They almost seemed to be floating.

"That was rough. I thought Chraft's guys were camels by the way they held their water," Mahmood said looking so much more relieved.

"Let's go, we need to catch up to them," Arslin said, starting the engine. They left the Shell station and got back on the road. Within minutes, they were back in sight of Ian, Abu, and Hasan.

CHAPTER 42

"So what's the next stop?" Abu asked Asil.

"We're going to stop in Erzincan, which is about four hours away," Aslin replied.

"How often do you make the trip to Ararat?" Abu asked.

"About four times a year. You Americans seem to have a fascination about the mountain and the ark," Asil said, looking at Ian and answering Abu at the same time.

"You can blame the reason we're here on my boss," Hasan said, looking up from the newspaper he bought at the gas station.

"Oh yes, a Mr. Chraft. Ibrahim told me about him. He must be a very rich man to send you over here to look for something that no one really knows exist," Asil replied.

"His family owns a trucking company back in the states. He is paying us out of his inheritance to find the ark." Ian replied back to Asil.

"Must be a huge inheritance for him to pay all of you to do this, as the tourists we get aren't that wealthy, but they aren't throwing that kind of money around either. That man must really believe the ark is up there." Asil said to Ian with a raised eyebrow.

You have no idea. Hasan thought to himself and went back to reading the paper he had bought at the gas station.

"So, tell me more about this guy. What does he do besides sending three guys on a search for a boat that's supposedly on a mountain top?" Asil said to Ian.

"He is a politician back in the States. Hasan works for him. He told us about the senator, then we went to meet him, and now here we are—in a van on the Turkish autobahn on our way to go up a mountain top to look for a boat that is supposedly up there," Ian answered him. "And by the way, Asil, why did Ibrahim tell you about Chraft? No one is supposed to know about us except him. Swanson knows about us, too, but that is another story," Ian said, questioning his driver. "I suppose Ibrahim didn't think anything of it as American politics don't mean anything to us here in Turkey. Except maybe to our politicians but they don't believe in the Bible or the ark. As far as they're concerned, you're just another expedition that asked for permission to climb the mountain and you got it. That doesn't always happen so be thankful for the opportunity," Asil replied to Ian.

Ibrahim had already told them about all the stories of the expeditions that have gone up there and how some have claimed to see the ark, where others have only brought back stories. Ian was tired of hearing about how much like idiots they looked like for going on this trek.

"I am sorry if I have offended you, Dr. James, I did not mean to. As I said, Americans seem to have a fascination with the mountain and the ark. Yours, along with other

American presence here, has proven this time and time again. I apologize," Asil said to him.

"Don't worry about it, Asil. We should be used to this whole thing by now, but I guess the thought of actually finding a biblical artifact is very intriguing," Ian replied back.

"Exactly," Asil said, looking at Ian and smiling. Ian knew Asil more than understood.

Hasan's cell phone rang.

"How are things, Hasan?" It was the voice of Senator Chraft. He had forgotten to call his boss before they left Ibrahim's house that morning.

"We just made a stop in Yozgat, Senator. We are now on our way to Erznincan. There we will stop again. Then we will push on to Igdir. There, we will stop for the night and meet our female guide, make sure everything is ready, and then head up the mountain."

"Female guide, huh? Excellent. How many times has she been up the mountain?"

"From what we have been told, she is very adept in being a guide, no worries."

"I see. Well, from what I'm seeing on the computer, Erzincan is quite a ways from Yozgat. It looks to be at least a ten-hour drive, but everything is okay, right?" Clayton asked as he Googled the city Hasan had just mentioned. Even though the senate was on August recess, he was keeping track of his men's whereabouts.

"Yes, all is well. I will call you from Erzincan," Hasan answered

"Good. How are Ian and Abu? How are they holding up?" Clayton asked.

"Just fine. We're good after the sorely needed pit stop."

"Excellent, call me when you get to your destination as well. Have you seen any of Swanson's men?"

"Not so far, but there were a couple of guys who seemed to be watching the house the morning I called you. But other than that, we have seen no one."

"Okay, just keep your eyes peeled and be careful. Swanson's men will stop at nothing until they stop you."

"Will do, Boss."

"Hasan, one more thing: God bless."

Hasan hung up and looked out the window as the Turkish countryside sped by. He was starting to feel a little bit excited.

"What'd the boss say, Hasan?" Ian asked, looking back at him from the front seat.

"He said to keep our eyes peeled for Swanson's guys and to be careful."

"You mentioned some guys watching us; when did this happen?"

"This morning when I made the phone call to Chraft."

"You didn't say anything about it to us."

"I didn't really know if they were watching us or how long they had been parked there. I was not going to assume anything."

"Well, now that you do mention it, I think keeping our eyes peeled would be a good thing," Ian said, turning to face forward. In both of their minds, Ian and Hasan assumed the men in the car somehow had a connection to Monty Swanson. Which also meant Swanson's men were indeed already on their trail.

Chapter 43

The next stop was the city of Erzincan, Turkey, a city with a population of 93,548. After this quick stop, they again got back on the road.

"Next and last stop, Igdir," Asil said. He was now starting to grow tired. He drained his coffee cup quickly to get the full impact of the caffeine. Although it was nothing like the real Turkish coffee he was used to drinking, it was all he had.

"And just think, we still have to go back to Ankara when this is all over," Abu said out loud to himself.

"How often did you say you make this trip, Asil?" Hasan asked.

"About four times a year," he replied, adjusting himself in his seat.

"You must get paid well enough to do so," Ian said.

"Let's just say I am well compensated for my time and effort," he said, grinning.

Senator Swanson's cell phone rang.

"Where're you boys, Mahmood?" he asked.

"We just pulled out of Erzincan. We're on our way now to Igdir, and we still have Chraft's guys well in sight."

"Have they seen you at all? Do they know you boys are on their trail?"

"They don't seem to. We pulled over after they left the gas station, and we are back on the road within fifteen minutes after they left."

"Mahmood, you're one heck of a man. I do hope Tyler is learning as much as he can from you. He's going to be my go-to guy when you're gone, whenever that might be."

"That might be sometime sooner than later, but we'll see what happens."

"Sure thing, Mahmood, no reason to make any rash decision right now. Call me when you get to Igdir. It's gonna start to get real exciting from there on out."

"Will do, Boss," he hung up the phone and stretched out on his seat for a nap.

"What did Uncle Monty say, Mahmood?" Tyler asked, looking back at him.

"I am to call him when we get to Igdir. Your uncle wants to make you his go-to guy after I am gone and for you to make this a very good learning experience."

"Are you going to be leaving after we get this done and back to the States?" Tyler asked with a look of caution on his face. Mahmood looked out the van's window and said nothing.

CHAPTER 44

The city of Idgir loomed large in front of them. It was nine at night, and the city was very well lit up. They were only fifteen minutes away from it coming off the E eighty eight.

"It's about time," Abu said, more than ready to get to Asil's house to shower and then go to bed.

"When do we meet our guide?" he asked Asil.

"Tomorrow morning. I will take you to her base camp in the foothills of the mountain. She will then take charge of you there," he said, answering Abu.

Asil pulled the van into the driveway of his apartment in the Igdir suburb of Yedi Kasim. The four men piled out of the van, grabbed their bags, and went inside the apartment. Asil had a small two-bedroom apartment and told them he would take the couch, and that they could decide for themselves which one got Asil's bed, the second bedroom and the living room floor. Hasan took Asil's bed, Ian the second bedroom, and Abu took the living room floor.

"The bathroom is the second left after the bedroom. Please make yourselves at home, and to give you a proper perspective, please, follow me," he said, turning to walk through his back door that led out of the kitchen and onto a small but comfortable patio.

"Mount Ararat is one hour in that direction. If it were daytime, you could see it very well from here," he informed them. Even though it was dark, the three of them started to feel more of a sense of accomplishment. They had come this far and were now standing only one hour away from the mountain and possibly the ark. It was all starting to come into focus.

"Are any of you hungry? I will make something quick before you go to bed," he asked them; even though all of them had an *I want to go to bed* look on their faces.

"I want a shower and the living room floor," Abu said, turning to go back through the patio door and down the hall to the shower.

"I think we're all just ready for bed, Asil," Ian said, also turning for the patio door.

"Very well. Breakfast will be at eight in the morning, and then I will take you to base camp. Get a good night's rest, gentlemen. It takes a strong heart to climb the mountain," Asil said to them, following them back through the patio door.

Arslin's cell phone rang.

"We are in the place. They are at Asil's apartment

in Yedi Kasim. We are outside and are keeping watch," Arslin's contact informed him.

"Very good," he responded back to him.

"My contacts have them in sight. They are staying in an apartment not far from where I live, which is only ten minutes away. They will watch them through the night. Get some rest, when we get home. It's going to get very busy starting tomorrow," Arslin informed Mahmood and Tyler.

Tyler turned to give Mahmood the *'are you ready for this'* look. He simply returned Tyler's look with a stone-cold gaze. Mahmood was more than ready.

CHAPTER 45

The morning sun rose over Mount Ararat with a brilliant glow. It was a cool but comfortable morning as Asil seated his guests around the table for morning breakfast. The men ate heartily, and talk was about the ark.

"Asil, do you believe the ark is up there?" Abu asked, taking a sip of coffee.

"I don't really know. I've never really wanted to go up the mountain to see. I guess I am more content driving tourists from Ankara to the mountain."

"So you're saying you've never had even the slightest wonder if it does exist?" Abu asked, sounding a little coy.

"I've heard more than enough stories. I don't need to climb a mountain to find out if a boat is up there. Besides, to be quite honest, I have a fear of heights," Asil admitted Abu.

"Well, that would be a very good reason to not climb the mountain," Abu said with a twinkle in his eye. Hasan excused himself from the table and walked out the patio door. A wondrous sight caught his eye. There before him stood the majestic Mount Ararat with the sun rising just above its peak. *It's so beautiful,* he thought to himself. *I do hope for all we have been through, the ark is indeed up there.* He opened up his cell phone and punched some numbers.

"Hasan, how are things?" Chraft's voice asked at the other end.

"I'm looking at the mountain right now. It's so beautiful with the sun rising up behind it," Hasan replied back.

"Imagine how Noah and his family felt after the forty days of rain were over and the flood water receded and they were finally able to leave the ark. What a glorious sunrise that too must have been," Chraft said, making Hasan's current image of the mountain seem even more beautiful.

"I can't even imagine," he replied back to Chraft.

Hasan's eyes were transfixed on the mountain.

"Gentlemen, we have to leave now. We are to rendezvous with Aliye in one hour," Asil informed them, grabbing his van keys and heading out the door.

"Aliye, she is our guide, yes?" Abu asked.

"Yes Abu. She is your guide," Asil responded, putting the key into the hole to open the door and getting into the van. All four men were now inside and putting their seat belts on.

"Are you still worried about having a female guide, Abu?" Ian asked with some concern in his voice.

"I know I should not be, but in my culture, women do not guide men up mountains; men guide men up mountains," he responded, trying not to sound arrogant. Although he was born in America, his father had instilled the culture of his homeland of Egypt deep within him.

"Relax, Abu, we've gotten this far. I'm sure whoever she is, she's more than capable. If Ibrahim can have confidence in her, why can't you?" Ian said to him, trying not to sound like he was admonishing his friend.

Abu nodded his head to let Ian know that was a good point.

Asil pulled out of his driveway and headed east toward Ararat.

"Let's go" Mahmood said to Arslin.

They had just watched Ian and the others leave for the mountain.

"Our guide will be ready, yes?" Mahmood asked, his voice sounding like a man who was ready for battle.

"He is ready—with everything." Arslin said.

The morning sun was higher now, and Mount Ararat looked larger the closer they got to it. Mahmood and Tyler arrived at Yesil Yayla base camp at the 16,843-foot level of the mountain. They were introduced to their guide, a Sherpa who looked like he was in his mid-thirties and had already seen more than his share of life. His name was Tenzin, and he shook hands with Mahmood and Tyler and got down to business.

"So, we finally meet. Are you ready to go up the mountain?" Tenzin asked them.

"Oh yes," Tyler said, sounding nervous but excited at the same time.

"Do you have our supplies?" Mahmood asked with a steely eyed gaze.

"I have everything you need. I will give it to you at the appropriate time," Tenzin said as another guide appeared—a woman who was small in stature but had a large smile on her face.

"Hi, I'm Aliye. So nice to meet you," she said, her voice sounding very pleasant. "Where is the other guy?" she asked Mahmood and Tyler, not yet realizing that this was not her group.

"Other guy?" Tyler asked, looking confused and maybe a little bit cautious.

"I was told there would be three of you. Ian, Abu, and Hasan," she responded.

"They are obviously not here yet. But let's go inside the tents you'll be staying in, and I will get you oriented to your surroundings," Tenzin said to Tyler and Mahmood. Aliye watched them as they stowed their gear, and Tenzin began telling them about the mountain and their present location. She walked over to where the pack animals were standing and rechecked the bags of provisions each animal was carrying. While she was checking the animals, another van pulled up. Asil parked the van and Ian, Abu, and Hasan all climbed out. Asil waved at Aliye, who walked over to greet the newly arriving guests.

"You must be Ian, Abu, and Hasan. So nice to meet you," she said.

"Nice to meet you, Aliye," Ian said, extending his hand to hers.

"Oh, you know my name already," she said, sounding surprised.

"Asil told us who you were," Abu said, casting a gaze from the top of her head down to the soles of her mountain-boot-wearing feet. To Abu, Aliye was indeed a sight to behold. At five feet five inches tall, her jet black hair was pulled into a pony tail, and its length fell to her mid-back. Abu noticed she was also voluptuous and very athletically built. The fact that she also had liquid blue eyes held his fascination as well. Abu had not seen a mountain girl this beautiful. He was caught completely off guard.

"We should walk over to the tents, so I can orient you to where you are and tell you a little about this mountain," she said, motioning for them to follow her. As they followed her to the tents, Ian caught a glimpse of a familiar-looking man out of the corner of his eye. He saw Mahmood, who was also staring right back at him. Ian stopped in his tracks to get better look at the man standing in the distance. Yes, it was most definitely him. Ian noticed Mahmood's stare was full of contempt, and his body language was not that far behind. His arms were crossed against his chest and his face showed no emotion. To drive his point home, he put fore and middle fingers to his eyes, and then pointed to Ian with his forefinger. A gesture that told Ian, *I'm watching you.* Ian caught up with his group as Aliye was showing them both the packhorses they would be riding up the mountain.

"Have any of you ever been on a horse?" she asked in a matter-of-fact tone of voice.

Each man looked at the other and shook his head that none of them in fact had ever been on a horse.

"I've seen a lot of them on television; does that count?" Abu responded, trying to be cool. Ian and Hasan gave him a sideways glance that said, *Abu, don't.*

"If this were a Hollywood production of a western movie, then absolutely, that would count. But this isn't Hollywood, Abu," Aliye said to him, being very nice and warm in her response. "Well, don't worry. These animals are completely accustomed to people, so our ride should be very smooth," she added.

"How long have you been doing this?" Hasan asked.

"Quite a few years, but please, don't worry. I know what I'm doing," she answered.

"How old are you?" Abu asked, really questioning whether or not she did indeed know what she was doing.

"Old enough to take all of you up this mountain," she said, tugging harder on the horses' saddle strap, making it tighter and making the horse whinny. She patted the horse on its side and loosened the strap a notch. She turned to face Abu but was talking to all of them. She spoke with respect and determination.

"Gentlemen, I realize you're not used to being guided by a woman. But you also need to realize none of you are from here. I was raised in the foothills of this mountain, so that makes me very familiar with the landscape. I also realize that to you I am not very tall and don't look old enough to take any of you anywhere. I'm a little older than what you think, and I have also ridden these foothills all my life. So can we get past the fact that I am a woman, and I'll get you a little farther up the mountain to the next base camp? You'll be spending a few more days there to acclimatize yourselves to the mountain."

Abu and Hasan were both stunned.

"Well said," replied Ian.

Asil turned to leave and go back to the van. He was done here. Hasan leaned in toward Aliye to ask her about supplies.

"Do you have everything we asked for?"

"I have everything I usually bring, plus a few more things extra. You will be very well taken care of," she assured him, looking him straight in the eye.

Tenzin, Mahmood, and Tyler then walked over to where the rest of them were standing.

"We should leave for the higher base camp. I'll take us the rest of the way," Tenzin said to her and the rest of the group.

"You're right. Mount up, everyone. We have a journey ahead of us," she said, telling all the men to get on the horses. They mounted their steeds, and Tenzin lead the way up the trail to the next camp with Tyler and Mahmood in tow, followed by Aliye, Ian, Hasan, and Abu bringing up the rear. Hasan rode up next to Aliye and, as quietly as he could, informed her that he needed both the satellite phone and the global positioning system tonight when they got to base camp. He needed to make a phone call, and his cell phone would not work at these altitudes. Aliye replied that she would give him everything he needed at the base camp.

Chapter 46

They arrived at camp two that afternoon. They dismounted the horses and proceeded to set up the area where they would be spending the next couple of days. Aliye set up by her group; Tenzin set up by his as they were all next to each other. Mahmood and Ian exchanged glances as they put up their tents. Finally, Ian could no longer tolerate Mahmood's presence within the camp.

He would like to converse with Mahmood quietly and tactfully, but he knew this was impossible.

"Mahmood, why are you here?" he asked, hoping to coerce him into admitting his real reason for being there. Mahmood did not take the bait.

"For the same reason you are, maybe to catch a glimpse of the ark," he responded back, being careful with his words.

"Then why do you want to kill us for photographing it and bringing the evidence back to the States?" Ian demanded.

"*What?* Kill you for taking pictures of the ark? What does that mean?" Aliye asked, stunned from Ian's accusation. Everyone stopped what they were doing to listen to this discussion. Tenzin remained silent.

"Aliye, we know who this guy is," he said pointing to Mahmood. "He was sent here to kill us to prevent the taking of those pictures of the ark. He'll kill us all, and then they will go back down the mountain as if nothing happened. Go on, ask him yourself," Ian demanded of her.

"Is this true, Abu, Hasan?" she asked them both. They both nodded their heads in agreement. "Is this true, Mahmood?" she asked, confronting him.

"Is this how you make friends, Dr. James?" Mahmood asked Ian in a mocking tone.

"You two know each other?" Aliye asked, wondering if indeed Ian's accusation might be true.

"Oh yes, we know each other. We've had the unfortunate luck to have met the first time on a dig in Egypt. The other time was during a late-night car chase on the streets of Washington D.C. on the way to the airport. We were sent here to document the ark; he was sent here to stop us. And I don't know who this other guy is," Ian exclaimed, pointing to Tyler.

"Mahmood, I will ask you one more time: is this true?" Aliye asked him, confronting him again.

He looked at her in a very condescending way. He said nothing as he turned to walk past Tenzin toward his horse. Mahmood reached into a saddlebag and pulled out the Glock 9mm handgun. He pointed it directly at Ian.

"Well, I guess now is as just a good of a time as any. Yes, I'm going to kill all of you. When I do a job, I hate having to deal with any witnesses. It makes things messy, legalistic, and time consuming. With the exception of my two friends, none of you will leave this mountain!" he said, motioning to Tyler and Tenzin.

"Did you know about this, Tenzin?" Aliye asked him, not believing Mahmood's statement.

He said nothing as he brought his gaze from her to the mountain. She walked over to him and looked him in the eyes.

"Look at me, and tell me you knew nothing about this," she said to him, a surprising air of calmness in her voice.

Tenzin turned around and walked a few feet ahead. He nodded his head as he turned again to face her.

"Yes. Yes, I did know about this! You're obviously not tired of bringing over-privileged American tourists up here to either climb the mountain or go look for a mythical boat. I want more. I don't plan on living in that village we grew up in. I'm sick of it and this mountain. I had an opportunity and I took it. I'm going to get away from here for good!"

Aliye balled up her right fist and punched Tenzin in the face, knocking him to one knee.

"I have family who expects to see me home after this tour!" she screamed at him as he stood back to face her.

She attempted to punch him again. He grabbed her wrist and shoved her to the ground. Abu was stunned, but Hasan and Ian started to move forward to see if she was all right. Mahmood pointed the gun at the both of them.

"Let us see if she is all right!" Ian demanded.

"She is okay; she is still breathing. Back away!" Mahmood commanded.

Ian and Hasan did as they are told. Mahmood pointed the gun at Aliye.

"Get up!" he demanded, his voice seething with rage. Aliye rose to her feet. She slapped the sides of her pants to get the dirt off.

"Do you know where the ark is?" he asked her, his impatience growing by the minute.

She took a breath before speaking.

"I have heard it is on the northwestern slope, which is near the mountain's summit. I have not seen it, but I have been to the summit many times. The last two summers have been very hot. Maybe we'll get lucky and see something," she told him, gesturing that she did not really know.

"Tomorrow you will take us there. Don't try to slip back down the mountain. We're sleeping right next to you, and I have very good hearing. I also don't sleep very well and tend to shoot at strange noises during the night. All of you will stay in your tent. We leave at first light," Mahmood informed her of what she was going to do whether she wanted to know or not.

Tyler, Tenzin, and Mahmood retired to Tenzin's tent to discuss tomorrow mornings activities. Night fell as the sun slipped behind the mountain.

Chapter 47

Quietly, all three men slipped into Aliye's tent.

"Are you okay?" Hasan asked with concern in his voice. Aliye was laying in her sleeping bag, tears running down her cheeks.

"I've known Tenzin all my life. I can't believe he would do this to me," she said, burying her face in her hands. "My parents died several years ago. My grandmother raised me. We're all that we have left. Being a guide is the only thing that supports us. She is eighty-five years old and is blind. When I'm up here, my brother takes care of her."

"Aliye, where is the GPS and the satellite phone?" Hasan asked her, putting his hand on her shoulder for comfort.

"They're in the saddlebag Abu is almost sitting on," she responded, lifting her face to him in appreciation of his touch.

"Sorry," Abu said shifting his weight so Hasan could pick it up. He reached inside the bag and retrieved the phone and the GPS. Then something else caught his sight. Aliye had two Glock 9mm guns and a very nice-looking machine pistol. Hasan was impressed.

"You've brought your own weapons. Do your tourists

always get violent?" he asked her with a twinkle in his eye. She allowed herself a small laugh. It felt good.

"No, The area where the ark is, that's bad territory. Kurdish rebels control that area. To them, the ark is considered sacred, and they don't like outsiders either looking at it or taking things from inside of it. When I come up this mountain, I am very much determined go back home."

"Is this mountain really that dangerous?" he inquired of her.

"Only when it comes to have anything to do with the ark. But it's not always that dangerous. And I like being prepared."

"Makes sense to me," Hasan responded.

He called Senator Chraft.

"Hello, Senator Chraft," Clayton answered. The word *unknown* came up on his screen. He figured it might be Hasan, so he answered anyway. He figured right.

"Senator, this is Hasan."

"At last, Hasan. Where are you guys now? I have been trying to reach you," Clayton said to him in a very concerned voice.

"You can't call me on my cell. Abu, Ian, and I are already halfway up the mountain. I am calling you from a satellite phone. I have a GPS, and I need the co-ordinates to the ark. We are going up there at first light."

"Is your GPS on right now?"

"Yes."

"Okay, this is the location: Thirty-nine degrees, forty-two minutes, ten seconds north. Then forty-four degrees, sixteen minutes, thirty-three seconds east. Or about at fifteen thousand five hundred feet. You got that?"

"Got it. We'll use the GPS to reel ourselves in."

"You could do that. But I've got a better idea. I'm going to call a friend of mine who is the executive director of a company called Digital Globe. They have a satellite that has taken several photos of the mountain. With her satellite and your GPS, both of those can get you there," Chraft said enthusiastically.

"Another female. If we do find it, then maybe we can start thinking about how we're going to get this thing off the mountain," Hasan said, being facetious.

"What does that mean?" Chraft asked.

"Boss, I'm joking. But she needs to call me tomorrow as soon as she can. And Senator Swanson's men are here with us as well. They are in the very next tent. And they have already made their intentions very clear to us. But I want you to know we have one heck of a guide with us. She brought us up here fully armed."

"Excellent. Now, go do what I sent you there to do. Above all else, stay safe as you can, and Hasan, you, Ian, and Abu do what you have to in order to stay alive. Understood?"

"Very well Mr. Chraft."

"I will have her call you as soon as possible. Her name is Kelly George. She will be a tremendous asset to this expedition."

"Got it Boss."

Hasan hung up and put the phone back in the saddlebag.

"What'd he say?" Abu asked.

"The senator knows someone who is the director of a company called Digital Globe. This person is going to call tomorrow, and between her satellite and this GPS, we're guaranteed to find the ark. If it in fact does exist."

Abu put his hand over his chin. *Another female*, he thought to himself. He thought about the cultural upbringing his father had given him. Although he still loved him, Abu knew he had to change his way of thinking about the role of females in society. Obviously, a strong woman was a good thing to have, period.

Hasan checked his watch. It was late, and they needed sleep. First light came early.

"We need to sleep, if that's possible. Let's go back to our tents. We don't need Mahmood shooting at strange noises in the middle of the night," Hasan said to the other men, rising to leave the tent. Aliye grabbed Hasan's leg.

"Stay with me tonight. I would feel better with some male company," she said to him.

The look in her eyes told him she needed his company. Although she was a strong woman, and she knew that about herself, she had already been betrayed by her childhood friend. She knew she could trust Hasan.

"I will," he said to her, but first I need to go and get my sleeping bag."

They got up and left the tent and Hasan returned seconds later and lay down opposite Aliye in her tent.

CHAPTER 48

"Hello?" Hasan said as he answered the satellite phone. His voice sounding like a man who was not yet awake.

"Is this Hasan I'm speaking to?" the female voice on the other end asked.

"Yes. Who am I speaking to?" he answered back.

"Hasan, I am Kelly George. I am president and chief executive officer of a company called Digital Globe. Clayton Chraft called me last night and told me the details of what's been going on. I will tell you we have taken many satellite photos of Mount Ararat, but each time, the cloud cover had been so thick that we can't see anything," she informed him.

Hasan checked his watch; it was four in the morning. He looked over at Aliye, she was leaning on one elbow listening to the conversation.

"You say that you have a satellite, and you have already taken pictures of this mountain?" He was now fully awake. Aliye was putting her boots on.

"Yes, we have," Kelly answered back.

"Can you see the mountain now?" he asked her excitedly. Right now, he could not get enough information.

"No, not right now. We are not online with the

satellite right now, and it's not over your area as of yet," she informed him.

"Tell me about this satellite of yours," he requested of her, poking his head out of the tent to see if anyone else was awake yet. The moon was still high, and he could still see some stars. They were the only ones awake.

"We have a satellite we named QuickBird. Right now, it's on a two hundred and ninety-mile-high orbit above the earth. When we want to, we can focus the satellite lens on an object as small as two feet across."

"Then you should have no problem seeing the ark. It's bigger than two feet," he said to her trying not to sound facetious. "I have a handheld global positioning system. Can you lock your satellite onto me and guide us to the ark?" he asked her as he was getting his things together.

"We can't lock onto you, but we can feed you the coordinates from the satellite and guide you in," she informed him.

"How come I've never heard of you?"

"Have you ever seen Google Earth online jpegs?"

"Yes."

"That's us." Now, he understood.

"How soon can you have your satellite over this mountain?" he asked.

"Well, we would have to raise its orbit from a low-earth one to that of a geosynchronous one or a high-earth orbit. And position it over the mountain in a stationary orbit. What time is it there?"

"It's almost five a.m."

"Give us ninety minutes, and we'll have the QuickBird over your area," she told him.

"Okay, I will call you in ninety minutes," he replied and hung up.

"Between you, me, and those weapons you brought with you, we will get to that ark and then get off this mountain," he said, talking to Aliye. Hasan put the two 9mm Glocks in the leather holsters that were in the same saddlebag and the machine pistol went into her back pocket. He also handed her a holster with a Glock and two magazines full of ammunition. She loaded one magazine and chambered a round. Hasan did the same.

CHAPTER 49

"Everybody up!" Mahmood barked from outside his tent. Tyler walked around slapping the outer shell shells of everyone's tent with his hand.

"Let's go, everybody! Up, up, up!" he bellowed, echoing Mahmood's command.

Everyone climbed out of their tents and walked toward the horses. Mahmood noticed the backpacks slung over Hasan and Aliye's shoulders.

"What's in the backpacks?" he demanded, unzipping them to check their contents.

"The same things that are in Tenzin's backpack, Mahmood—extra gear. Or didn't he inform you of that after your little testosterone party last night?" she asked in an offensive manner.

He lifted his arm to backhand her but stopped.

"No, I'm going to enjoy killing you," he said to her. She was still looking at him defiantly, which made his blood boil and the thought of killing her that much sweeter.

"We leave in ten minutes! Tear everything down. Tenzin will lead us to the northwestern slope. We will be behind him, and you'll be behind us," he ordered.

"Mahmood, aren't you concerned with the Kurdish

rebels that patrol this area? They could kill us anytime they wanted to," Aliye asked him, trying to make him realize the seriousness of their situation.

"That won't happen, Aliye," Tenzin said, chiming into the conversation. "The rebels have been paid off. We've been in their territory since last night. If they were going to kill us, it would have happened then," he informed her.

"Ten minutes, people. Let's go!" Mahmood barked again.

Fifteen minutes later, the group was on their way to the northwestern slope. The sun was raising higher overhead, and as they looked around the mountain, it became even more beautiful. Ian glanced up at the summit and saw that it was still covered in snow. He wondered about this.

"Seems to me that if you've had two hot summers as you say you've had, there shouldn't be as much snow as that," he said to Aliye, pointing at the mountaintop.

"Ian, it would take at least a decade of straight, dry, hot summers to melt all that ice and those glaciers. The summit of Ararat is perpetually covered in snow. Just so you know, this mountain is pretty much an extinct volcano. From the fourteen to seventeen thousand-foot level, much of the lava fields are covered in snow. We're talking about an area that covers seventeen square miles, and the snow and ice cap is up to three hundred feet deep," she informed him.

"Do you really think the ark came to rest on this mountain, Aliye?" Abu asked.

"That's the story, Abu. There have been many

expeditions up here. Some claim to have seen it, some not. But there has never been any proof of its existence. Except of course, word of mouth."

"I think it would be awesome for us actually find it," Abu replied.

"So would I, but the upper reaches of the mountain are covered with broken lava rock. It's so difficult to get there because of that. But yet, this is the mountain that has most of the reported eyewitness accounts. Because of those accounts, that's really the only reason people still come here," she finished. Abu's curiosity was satisfied.

"Tenzin, what are they talking about back there?" Tyler asked. He kept turning around to see them talk to one another.

"She is just explaining more about the mountain and ark sightings to them. In her case, it's once a tour guide, always a tour guide," he answered Tyler, rolling his eyes and shaking his head.

"But doesn't glacial ice move?" Hasan asked her.

"From what I understand, yes. But there is really only one legitimate glacier on this mountain, and that is the black glacier. And yes, one would think that if the ark is under a glacier it would be ground to bits. But having said that, roughly ninety percent of the supposed eyewitness accounts claim the ark was sticking out of the ice. But none of them saw the same boat-like structure. Some have claimed it looked like a barge, some claim a boat. Others claim it's in one piece, still others say it's broken into three or four pieces. With more eyewitness accounts than evidence, no one really knows," Aliye said, finishing her talk and taking a drink of water from her canteen. They continued to climb higher and higher. Even though the sun was now almost directly overhead, a cool breeze was blowing, which brought the temperature down a little.

"Mahmood, I suggest we stop long enough to put our coats on," Aliye yelled to him.

"It is a little cool," Tyler said, hugging himself to stay warm.

"Five minutes' rest. How much farther to the summit, Aliye?" he asked, pulling his horse up next to hers.

"We're not far from it. But when we reach the snowfields, we'll have to leave the horses behind."

"How much longer until we reach the snowfields?"

She noticed he was calmer now and not as wound up as he was last night. She still did not allow her guard down.

"If you look up there, you'll see the beginning of the snowfields," she told him, pointing just a little farther up the mountain.

"When we get to there, we have to leave the horses and go the rest of the way on foot. The summit is an hour climb from there."

"And how do we know the horses will still be here when me, Tenzin, and Tyler get back?" he asked, reminding her of his plans.

"These horses belong to us, and they know to stay in place while we're gone." She informed him. Satisfied, he returned to the front of the line.

"You could've talked to me about that," Tenzin said to him, feeling a little offended.

"I wanted to remind her they will not be coming back," he retorted. Mahmood saw everyone had coats on now.

"Let's go!" he yelled, and they once again began to climb. The snowfields were inching closer.

CHAPTER 50

An hour later they reached the snowfields. They got off the horses, and Aliye and Tenzin threw blankets over them to keep them warm. Then they tied them together. A thick fog began rolling across the snowfield.

"Okay, we have to tie ourselves to each other for safety reasons. You guys already know how to use the crampons in case you slip and start to slide," Tenzin informed them. The group tied themselves together and began up Mount Ararat to its summit. Hasan's satellite phone rang. Mahmood spun around and glared at him. Aliye almost drew her gun on him.

"Hello, Hasan here," he said, speaking into the mouthpiece.

"Hi, Hasan. Everything okay?" Kelly asked cautiously. He had sounded like he was winded.

"Oh yes, everything is fine. We're now climbing up to the mountain's summit. We should be there in what, another thirty minutes?" he replied, asking Aliye and answering Kelly at the same time.

"Forty-five to be more accurate," Aliye said back to him.

"Okay, forty-five minutes. But I can look right

above me and see the summit," he said, trying to sound enthusiastic.

"How is the weather there now?" Kelly asked him.

"Can't you see from the satellite?"

"From up here, it looks a little foggy as usual. But how does it look from your perspective?" she asked him.

"Well, we're on the snowfield just below the summit. There is a fog cloud rolling across us right now. It's not that thick, but there are breaks in the cloud. So I would think you might be able to visualize the mountain top," he replied.

"Very well then. We have the satellite over your location, and everything looks fine." She told him.

"Awesome," he responded.

"I will call you back when and if we see anything," she said to him and hung up.

Mahmood was still staring at him.

"So, you have a satellite phone. Who were you talking to just now?" he asked Hasan as he walked up to him.

"I was talking to someone who can guide us to the ark."

"I see. So are we close to the ark? Are we in the general area? Where is the ark?" Mahmood said, wanting an answer from Hasan.

"Mahmood, I already told you where it might be, and there is still no guarantee it's there!" Aliye responded, trying to calm him down by putting her hand on his arm. Mahmood angrily shook her hand from his arm, and Aliye took a step back.

"Mahmood, calm down. They're going to call me

back if they see anything," Hasan said to him, looking Mahmood in the eyes.

"What stops you from killing us right now, Mahmood? You said you were not going to allow us to take pictures of it." Hasan said, questioning him on what his motives now were. Hasan knew Mahmood could kill them all right now and no one would know the difference. At least for a few more days.

"I am going to let you take pictures of the ark as per Monty Swanson's orders. And then I will confiscate everything you have. And if this ark is on a ledge or cliff, I am going to line you all up and kill you, letting each of you fall from it one by one. I will bring the pictures back with me and I will show Monty Swanson more pictures of the ark. Then we will have a drink in his office to mourn your deaths. The photos will be put on a disc and locked away forever," he said to Hasan. They're futures didn't look to bright at this point in time.

"Have you really ever killed anyone before Mahmood? And if not, will you be able to do so when the time comes?" Tyler said, looking at his partner curiously. Mahmood looked at Tyler and then walked over to him. He got really close to Tyler's face.

"Tyler, you would be amazed at what I am able to do when and if I need to do it. You don't know who I am or where I come from or where I've been. Your Uncle Monty knows me all too well and that's why he has every confidence in the world that when he needs me to do something, there will no loose ends to clean up," he said to Tyler just as calmly as if he were speaking to his own mother.

"Don't you think we should call Uncle Monty?" Tyler asked Mahmood.

"No, we'll call him after we get back down to base camp and let him know the job's done," Mahmood replied back to Tyler, who was now wondering whether not he should have accompanied Mahmood on this trip.

"Enough talking Tyler, we need to get to the summit and then the northwestern slope and we're burning too much daylight down here," he said gesturing for all of them to get moving.

"Let's go," Tenzin said to them.

Chapter 51

They reached the summit and stopped to catch their breaths. It was still foggy, and from up here, it looked almost twice as thick as from down below.

"What's the deal with all this fog?" Abu asked. He was bent halfway over with his hands on his knees.

"It's called upslope fog. It forms when the winds blow air up a slope, such as the one we're on now. It causes warm air to cool as it rises. The moisture in that air condenses to form this fog," Tenzin informed Abu.

"It's thick, but as it rolls by, you can see breaks in it," he added.

"Aliye, which way to the northwestern slope?" Hasan asked. She pointed in the appropriate direction.

"How long is the walk?" Mahmood asked, starting to catch his breath.

"Looks like maybe thirty minutes," she answered. She was not breathing so hard now.

"Let's go," Mahmood ordered. They began walking when the satellite phone rang.

"Hasan here," he answered.

"Hasan, we have a visual on the mountain. It's spotty,

but we're guessing there may be a cloud cover. What are the coordinates of the ark?" Kelly asked him.

"It's a fog bank, Kelly. It's not too thick, plus there are occasional breaks in it. We are now walking toward the northwestern slope. The coordinates are thirty-nine degrees, forty-two minutes, ten seconds north. Forty-four degrees, sixteen minutes, thirty-three seconds east," he said answering her.

"Okay, we got it. Stay on the line. We're going to send signals down to your GPS."

"I'm not hanging up," he responded back. His GPS began to light up. The LED pointer began to point in several different directions. A few seconds later, it pointed in the direction of the northwestern slope.

"I got the signal! Can you see anything?" he said excitedly into the mouthpiece.

"We can see you, and you're almost on top of your location," Kelly answered.

"How does the fog bank look from the satellite?"

"It looks like a milky haze with holes in it—stop! You're about to walk over a ledge!" Kelly screamed into Hasan's ear. The group froze in their tracks.

"Hey, what's that?" Kim Bostic, Kelly George's assistant, asked. Kim was at the computer and online with the satellite.

"Hasan, we caught a glimpse of something on the ledge below you. It's about one hundred feet down. Can you get to it?" Kelly asked him.

"What did you see, Kim?" Kelly asked her assistant.

"You're going to think I'm crazy, but it looked wooden.

I only got a half second glimpse, but it almost looked like boat!" she said incredulously.

"Hasan, I'm going to put you on speaker. Can you hear me?" she asked, now standing over her phone.

"Yes, I can hear you," he replied.

"Can you climb down the ledge?" she asked him again.

"She wants to know if we can climb down the ledge. They see something down there!"

Tenzin carefully peeked over the ledge. "We can, but we have to be extremely careful! This thing will not forgive us our mistakes!" he answered Hasan.

"Kelly, we can get down it, but it will take a little time." Hasan told her.

"Be careful, Hasan. It looks pretty unforgiving." she responded.

"Over here! We can go down this crevasse. We need to use our crampons and be careful!" Tenzin yelled. The wind was picking up. They began to climb down the crevasse on their way to the ledge below. In ten minutes, they were perched on it.

"We don't have much room. Looks like only about forty feet of walking space and another one hundred feet down to a more slanted slope!" Tenzin informed them.

"There it is; there it is!" Kim shouted. On the computer screen in front of her, in high resolution, was a wooden structure jutting out of the glacial ice.

"Hasan, do you see it?" Kelly yelled in his ear.

"No, there is a real thick blanket of fog now. We're

afraid to move as we don't have a lot of walking space down here. What do you see?"

"You're facing the wrong way! Turn around; it'll be right in front of you!" she exclaimed.

Ian turned. He was thunderstruck. There in front of him, during a break in the fog, stood the remains of Noah's ark. *It does exist* he said as he could only mouth the words to himself as he fell to his knees. Hasan let the satellite phone drop from his grasp. Aliye covered her mouth with her hands. Abu could do nothing; he was too stunned. Mahmood and Tyler could only stare in disbelief. The ark; it was there, just as the Bible said it was. The ark in all its wooden, pitch-covered, frozen glory, sat where it came to its final resting place over four thousand years ago.

"Ian, start taking pictures!" Hasan yelled to him above the wind. He had managed to unglue himself long enough to yell at Ian. Ian had a two-gigabit card for his digital cameras and plenty of batteries. He was about to fill one up and kill the other.

"Aliye, here, take the disc recorder and start filming everything!" he hollered to her over the wind.

"Kelly, are you seeing this?" Hasan yelled into the phone after realizing he had dropped it.

Neither Kim nor Kelly could speak, their hands were over their mouths, and they were in their seats. They were indeed seeing this. The ark was right in front of them on the computer screen.

"Hey, there's a door!" Aliye exclaimed as she used the camera's zoom feature to get a closer shot.

"Let's go inside the ark!" Ian exclaimed. The four of them started walking toward the ark.

"Stop! Don't go any farther! Give me the cameras!" Mahmood screamed at them. He had freed his weapon from his back pocket and was pointing it directly at Ian.

"Mahmood, are you crazy?! The ark, it's right there! It *does* exist. Uncle Monty was wrong; I thought he was just being crazy, but now I know he was serious. But he is still wrong. Drop the gun, and let's go inside this thing and explore it!" Tyler implored Mahmood. This was a once-in-a-lifetime chance, and he knew it. Mahmood balled up his right fist and punched Tyler in the face. Tyler took a few steps back to keep his balance. Through the pain, he could see the absolute look of determination on Mahmood's face.

"Mahmood, stop it!" Hasan demanded. Mahmood trained the gun on Hasan. Tyler had enough. He lunged at Mahmood, attempting to grab the weapon out of his hand. They struggled with each other as one wanted the weapon, but so did the other. A shot rang out and a look of shock and horror came across Tyler's face. He grabbed Mahmood's shoulder and began dropping to his knees, coating Mahmood's coat with blood. Tyler collapsed at Mahmood's feet. While this was happening, Hasan had drawn his gun as had Aliye.

"Mahmood, I don't want to kill you, but I will if I have to! Give me your gun and walk away!" Hasan instructed Mahmood, who now had his gun trained on Hasan and Aliye. Hasan's patience was gone.

"Mahmood, you're outnumbered and outgunned. You're only option is to give up!"

"No! I have another option!" Mahmood said, taking a step toward Hasan. Another shot rang out. A look of pain and anguish came over Mahmood's face. He dropped to his knees still holding the gun. His last gaze was toward Aliye. The look on his face changed from pain to utter hatred. He collapsed beside the body of Tyler.

"What do we do now?" Abu asked.

"We go inside the ark! We do what we came here to do!" Ian bellowed.

"What about them?" Tenzin screamed.

"What about them? We're on top of a mountain in Turkey staring at a four thousand-year-old ark. If you want to mourn them, go right ahead!" Hasan said, turning to walk toward the ark. The other three followed Hasan's lead. Tenzin could only look down at the dead bodies of Mahmood and Tyler. His ticket out of being a guide and getting out of his small village had just died with these men.

CHAPTER 52

The ark was cavernous inside. A little ambient daylight could only penetrate a few feet inside the door of the ark, but it was enough for them to get their bearings. Hasan lifted the satellite phone to his ears.

"Hello?" he said, but there was no answer. The moment he stepped inside the ark, his connection was terminated. Ian and Aliye pulled the extra flashlights out of their backpacks and handed them to Abu and Hasan.

"Where's Tenzin?" Aliye asked. They looked around and called his name. Abu looked outside the ark's door. There were now three bodies on the snow-covered ledge instead of two.

"He decided to join them," Abu remarked to the others as he pointed to Tenzin's body.

"Okay, people, let's focus. We have an ark to document," Ian said as they began to shine their flashlights around the ark's insides.

"This film is from inside Noah's ark—" her voice trailing off as she checked her watch for the date and time. "August 23, 2008."

"It's now two p.m.," Ian said, picking up where she left off.

"Abu, Hasan, shine your flashlights over there," Ian requested. What looked like a black hole were two enormous cages. Their large iron doors were still open. The camera flash went off, lighting up the whole area.

"What do you suppose was kept in here?" Abu asked.

"I'm guessing elephants," Aliye remarked as she pointed the Blu-ray disc recorder toward the open cages, its light flooding them. As they walked farther into the ark, the sound of snow and ice crunching was heard under their feet as was the sound of running glacial water. As they continued to explore the ark, they shined their flashlights above them. On the second level, there was something that looked like what used to be a walkway. They saw more cages and what was probably petrified food still on the floors of some of them. There were wooden bowls full of frozen water. Whether that too was four thousand years old or from the glacier the ark was partially encased in was anyone's guess.

Aliye walked into one of the cages as something large and pitch black on the floor caught her attention. She pointed her camera toward it and pushed the zoom lens for a close up. Abu followed her in.

"What do you suppose this is?" Abu pointed his flashlight at it to get a better look.

"Unless I miss my guess, its animal feces," he replied.

He saw a wooden ladle on the table opposite him. He walked over the picked it up. He walked back over, bent down, and tapped the pile three times.

"Hard as a rock," he said, looking into the camera.

"Hello!" Hasan shouted from what sounded like a

hundred feet away, his voice bouncing off the cavernous walls of the ark. Everyone else pointed their flashlights and camera toward the sound of his voice. Aliye shot a close-up of him.

"I was wondering if it would echo in here," he said, shrugging his shoulders.

"What time is it, Abu?" Aliye asked.

"It's three thirty now," he answered.

An hour and a half had gone by in the twinkling of an eye.

"How many pictures have you taken, Ian?" she asked.

"Two hundred and fifty," he replied to her. She nodded her head.

"I filled the disc up. We have to leave now and get back down to camp two. It will be dark soon enough," she said with a voice of concern.

"Can't we just stay in here? We have shelter," Abu asked, already knowing the answer and why.

"Of course not. It does sound interesting, but we don't have food or a way to stay warm, and the weather on this mountain changes constantly. We have to leave now," she answered him, walking toward the door of the ark. They went outside; the fog was getting thicker.

The satellite phone rang.

"Hasan here," he answered into the mouthpiece with a raised voice.

"It's there, isn't it? The ark, it's there!" Kelly said excitedly in his ear.

"Yes, it is. Were you able to take any photos?" he asked.

"Oh yes! We took twenty, and they leave absolutely no doubt as to its existence. We zoomed in so close we could actually count the timbers!" she said, not able to contain her excitement.

"That's awesome. We're leaving the ark now because the fog is getting thicker, and it will be getting dark soon. Kelly, e-mail the photos to Clayton Chraft immediately. He needs to see them. Let him know we're on our way back down the mountain, and we will be in his office by midweek to show him what the inside of the ark looks like."

"We will," she replied. Hasan terminated the connection.

"What about the bodies?" Ian asked.

"Say a prayer for them. We need to leave. With as cold as it is up here, they'll be just fine. By midwinter they'll be covered by both ice and snow," Aliye said, digging her crampon into the ice wall in front of her. They climbed back up to the northwestern slope and retraced their footsteps back across the snowfield on the summit. They followed the same path all the way back down to where the horses were still waiting. They arrived at camp two an hour later and got set up for anther overnight stay. They barely slept that night as they kept looking at the pictures and film they took. Next morning, they got an early start and made their way back down to Yesil Yayla base camp. Asil was waiting for them over breakfast. They arrived during mid-meal. He got up to meet them and offer them something to eat.

"Good morning, Dr. James. Good morning, everyone. How was the climb?" he asked, hugging each of them.

"The most adventurous thing I've ever done," Ian responded with a smile. They all looked at each other with an understanding smile. It was quite the adventure. Asil asked about the other three men, and Aliye told him the whole story. Asil could not believe his ears as she described how evil of a man Mahmood was and how Tyler had tried to change his mind but how Mahmood would hear none of it. Asil then told Aliye that Tenzin had started to act strange in the couple of days before his party arrived. How he kept talking about leaving the village and maybe going to America. Asil told her that he just brushed it off as crazy talk, and that it was a comfortable living as a guide taking tourists up a mountain whose legend was biblical in nature. After breakfast, they said their goodbyes. Hugs were given all around.

"Can you come to Asil's place and spend the night? He makes a good dinner," Hasan asked Aliye.

"I'm sorry; I can't. As with the end of each tour, I have to get ready for the next one. That means bringing the horses off the mountain to rest them, feed them, and brush their coats. These horses work extremely hard taking people up this mountain," she said, looking at him. Asil and the other three climbed back into the van.

"It was very nice to have met you," Hasan said, looking into her eyes.

She took a step closer to him.

"It was nice meeting you as well," she said, looking up into his face. He took her into his arms and hugged her like he meant it, which he did. Asil, Abu, and Ian were watching from the van. Hasan and Aliye kissed each other passionately. It had already seemed like a lifetime had passed between them.

"Do you think you'll ever be back here?" she asked him, already starting to miss him.

"I could always come back here for another tour, go back up the mountain, and maybe see the ark again," he said, toying with her.

"Or maybe to come back here and see me?" she said to him with a playful look on her face. Hasan let out a little laugh.

"Okay, maybe to see you again, yes," he responded with a twinkle in his eyes and a smile on his face.

"I hate to break this up, you two, but we have to get going. These guys have a plane to catch on Tuesday," Asil said to them, leaning out the driver side window. Hasan took her hands in his. He raised them up to his lips and kissed both of them.

"Take care of yourself, Aliye."

"Take care of yourself, Hasan." They looked into each other's eyes.

"Ahem," Asil sounded, bringing Hasan back to reality.

"Okay, okay, I'm getting into the van," he said, letting go of Aliye's hands and walking past Asil to get inside the passenger side of the van. He climbed into the van, and the four of them drove off.

They all waved at her; Hasan touched his fingers to his lips, kissed them, and motioned toward Aliye, who repeated the gesture back to Hasan. Before long, they were out of sight.

"What are you going to tell Chraft about Mahmood and Tyler?" Ian asked with a raised eyebrow.

"The truth. I'll tell him exactly what happened and where. Then he can tell Swanson if he chooses to," he answered Ian.

They arrived back at Asil's apartment and unloaded themselves. They went inside and dropped their backpacks on the floor, and Ian promptly took a seat on the couch, Abu in the second bedroom, and Hasan sprawled himself on the floor. These men had just climbed Mount Ararat and came back down. They were exhausted and fell asleep within minutes.

CHAPTER 53

It was three o'clock on a beautiful Monday afternoon. Abu awoke first. He raised himself up in the bed and saw his clothes were still on. He rubbed his face with his hands and shook his head to get the cobwebs out. He took a deep breath and looked around the room. He remembered where he was. His feet felt lighter. He wiggled his toes and found that his boots had been taken off. He had the overwhelming urge to use the bathroom and swung his feet over the side of the bed feeling a thud against his feet.

"I found my boots," he said sleepily. He bent over and put his boots on, not bothering to tie them. He yawned heavily as he left the bedroom and turned to left and closed the bathroom door. Hasan began to stir. He opened his eyes and discovered he was looking at the floor. He turned his head and discovered that now he was also starting at his boots. He turned on his back and batted his heavy eyelids, which were full of sleep. He groaned as he raised himself upright also rubbing his face with his right hand. He heard a snoring noise on the couch. He looked over, and there was Ian; he was still asleep. Hasan laughed a little and then felt the urge to use the bathroom as well. He stood to his feet, not bothering to put his boots on.

He heard the commode flushing and then the door came open. He started down the hallway to the bathroom.

"You might not want to go in there," Abu warned him.

"I have to go so bad you don't even want to know," he informed Abu, closing the door. Abu heard Hasan coughing badly. *I warned you,* Abu thought to himself and shook his head. He looked at Ian who was still snoring on the couch. He looked down at Ian's feet. His boots were also off and were sitting at the edge of the couch. Abu looked around for Asil who was nowhere to be seen. He saw a note taped to the refrigerator.

Feel free to warm up the leftovers from last night. While you slept, I cooked you all something to eat. I will see you this evening. Hasan, call Chraft.

Abu opened the refrigerator door and looked inside. There were three plates covered with aluminum wrap. He picked one and took the wrap off and put it in the microwave. Hasan walked up behind him and took another plate out and put it on the countertop. The microwave signaled that Abu's food was hot. He took it out and walked outside the patio door and sat down at the table. Within a few minutes, Hasan sat next to him. He turned his cell phone on and dialed Chraft's number.

"Hasan, tell me everything!" Clayton Chraft said in a very excited tone of voice.

"Did Kelly e-mail you the satellite photos of the ark?" he asked Clayton through a yawn.

"Yes, and they are spectacular. The ark is right there in high resolution. I knew it was up there; the Bible does not lie!" Chraft said back to him. Hasan took a sip of the cup of tea he brought out with him. Asil has made a pot this morning before he left.

"How are you guys feeling? Is everything okay?" Chraft asked, calming down. He knew they must still be exhausted.

"Abu and I are up; Ian is still asleep," he said as Ian sat down at the table in front of him. He also had his breakfast plate with him.

"Or not," Abu chimed in.

"We're all okay, Senator. Still tired but okay," Hasan reported.

"Listen; take the rest of the day and just rest. Tomorrow, you have to get back to Ankara and catch the evening flight back. I'll meet with you Wednesday afternoon in my office where we'll download the pictures on a disc and look at the footage you shot also. This is so much worth the five million I am paying each of you."

"Just so you know, our guide's name was Aliye, and she shot the footage on a Blu-ray disc recorder."

"Did you thank her for me?"

"In a roundabout way yes. Also, Swanson's men are dead. Mahmood went totally crazy on us up there as we were about to go into the ark. It's a good thing Aliye likes guns. She packs them in a saddlebag when people want to go looking for the ark. They are not her regular tourists. Mahmood killed his buddy, Tyler, and then their guide, Tenzin, shot and killed himself as well. Aliye killed Mahmood. She saved our lives. I'm telling you this as you might also want to inform Swanson about his men," Hasan finished and took another bite of his food.

"That is a matter that must be handled very delicately. I will see to it," Chraft replied.

"Very well," Hasan answered.

"Get some more rest. I'll see all three of you Wednesday afternoon," Chraft told him.

Hasan hung up the phone and began to finish his meal.

The three of them began to share their experiences of the mountaintop. Hasan asked Abu if seeing the ark made him a believer. Abu replied that although he did in fact see Noah's ark, it went against his cultural upbringing. But he was still open to explore this further. Hasan agreed with him about this. He asked Ian the same question. Ian told Hasan he would have to revisit his roots in the faith.

"So, you guys are up, awake, and no worse for the wear and tear of mountain climbing, huh?" Asil asked, sitting down with a cup of tea.

"I don't think I'm going to go mountain climbing again," Abu replied. After having his life threatened by a manic like Mahmood, he knew his mountain climbing days were over.

"Ordinarily, our groups don't threaten their guides like Mahmood did. I could not believe a man would do that. But I'm glad you told me about that on the way back home," Asil said to him. "But tomorrow morning is going to come early for all of us. Your plane leaves Ankara tomorrow evening at six p.m. We will have to leave here at three a.m. if you're going to make your flight," he added.

"Well, I know I could use a shower and more sack time. So I'll shower and see you gentlemen at three a.m.," Ian said, rising to his feet. Abu, Hasan, and Asil sat and talked a while longer about anything that came to mind.

The ark continued to dominate the conversation. An hour later, all three rose from the table and went inside. Asil prepared another dinner while Abu and Hasan took the showers as well. At ten that night, they were all in bed. The morning would indeed come early.

CHAPTER 54

It was three in the morning and all four men were up, dressed, and ready to go. With cups of tea in hand, they climbed into the van, and Asil pointed the front of the van back onto the E-88 and back toward Ankara. The three of them mostly slept on the way back, but the times they were awake, Ian took pictures of the countryside. Abu filmed footage of it and each other. He also managed to film Hasan slap himself when Ian ran a finger across his cheek while Hasan was still sleeping. Asil blared the Turkish music on the radio while the other three created their own moves. It was five in the evening when Asil pulled the van into the passenger-unloading slot in front of Esenboga International Airport in Ankara. He let the van idle as he got out and said goodbye to his passengers. They shook hands and exchanged hugs and told Asil they would keep in touch. They waved goodbye to Asil as they walked inside the airport and checked in. The airline employee printed out their tickets and pointed in the direction of their departure gate. Getting past security, they stopped at a coffee shop for that beverage and a quick snack. Fifteen minutes later, they were seated at the gate for their flight that would leave in thirty minutes.

CHAPTER 55

"Good to see you again, Darrell," Ian said to Clayton Chraft's limousine driver. He had a look of curiosity on his face, and it was also mixed with a little doubt.

"Did you guys really see Noah's ark?" he asked really wanting to know.

"Didn't your boss show you the pictures?" Abu asked. He was really wondering why Darrell would even ask that question. Did Darrell really doubt them? They almost lost their lives in the process, and now he had the gall to ask them about it.

"I don't make it a habit to get on a United States senator's computer, Abu. That computer is government property. And besides, I don't know the password," Darrell replied, his voice sounding a little annoyed at the bluntness of Abu's question.

"It was a huge week for us, Darrell; don't mind Abu. We're still a little stunned and tired from it all," Hasan said to Darrell while looking at Abu.

"I'm sorry," Abu replied. "I guess if it were me, the first thing I would want to do is show those pictures to the world," he added.

"Forget it, Abu," Darrell told him. "Senator Chraft

most definitely plans on showing them to the world. But there is a certain way to do it, and Chraft is working on it right now," he finished.

"How?" Ian asked him.

"Ever hear of the Smithsonian Institution?" he replied, looking at Ian.

"So this is what Washington D.C. looks like in the daytime," Abu commented as they were on the way from their hotel room to Clayton Chraft's office.

CHAPTER 56

Up the elevator they went getting out on the fifth floor and turned left to go down the hallway. Stopping at the door with Senator Chraft's name on it, Darrell knocked twice, and he heard the senator invite them in.

"Gentlemen, welcome back, welcome back!" Clayton said excitedly as he shook each of their hands. He was giddy with excitement and did not bother to try and contain himself.

"First, thank you all so much for doing this for me. I can't truly express to you how grateful I am. But here is one way that I can," he said as he handed them each of their checks in the sum of the remainder of the agreed upon amount.

"Excuse me, gentlemen, have a seat please. I'm so excited, I forgot my manners. You're all millionaires now, and you deserve every penny that's written on those checks," he said, looking at them from across his desk.

"Darrell here tells us you're going to show the pictures at the Smithsonian. Just how many contacts do you have, if I can ask?" Abu asked.

"I don't know if I would call them contacts as I would call them friends. What you might not know, Abu, is that the Smithsonian Institution has seventeen members of the board of regents. I have a good relationship with all of them, and a really close one with a few. As a matter of fact, I play golf with the two top bosses on the board, the chief justice of the supreme court and the vice president of the United States, Christopher Daniels and Gerald Anthony respectively," he told Abu. Abu was impressed, and the look on his face showed it.

"I stand corrected. Not just them, also the secretary of the Smithsonian, Jeffery Allen," Clayton added.

"When do you talk to him about this?" Ian asked. The senator was very animated about the photos. Just how was Chraft going to set all of this in motion? Ian wondered.

"I already have. In six months, the new Noah's ark exhibition opens in the Sant Ocean Hall of the museum. But that's just the beginning. We are going to be breaking new ground on a new museum here in Washington. A museum dedicated to biblical archeology, and the Noah's ark exhibit is going to its first and permanent resident. And I've already spoken to the mayor, Abu, and we would very much appreciate it if you would be that museum's curator. Are you interested?" Clayton asked, smiling at Abu who was also smiling back and nodding that, yes, he most certainly would be interested.

"Dr. James, your specialty is Egyptology, correct?" he asked Ian.

"That's correct, Senator. I'm mostly interested in the pharaohs," Ian replied.

"You did know that there were quite a few of them

who interacted with Abraham, Joseph, and Moses?" Chraft said, acting like he had big news for Ian.

"Of course, I was doing research on one of them when I got a phone call from a certain someone in this room," he said, looking at Abu.

"Awesome, well, I'll again thank you all and invite you to the grand opening of the ark exhibit when it opens in October. I'll see that Darrell sends you the invitations," Chraft said, rising from his desk.

"I have to end this meeting as I have legislation to submit to my peers. Darrell will walk you out and take you back to your hotel. By the way, Dr. James, I know a man, a very good friend of mine, who is working a dig in Armania, Egypt. I told him about you, and he would very much like for you to fly down and be chief archeologist on the site. He unfortunately had a death in the family and will no longer be able to work the site. I took the liberty of both telling him that you would be interested, and I gave him your contact information. He is going to call you this Friday."

"How do you know my contact information?" Ian asked him.

"Dr. James, I'm a United States senator, and I have people. But don't worry; your e-mail and phone number are the only information he knows about you, besides what I have already told him," Clayton informed Ian. He thanked them once again and Darrell took them back down to the car and back to the hotel. Each man flew back home. Sure enough, like clockwork, six months later, they each had written invitations to the grand opening of the ark exhibit.

They were all back on a plane and back in Washington a week before the opening.

CHAPTER 57

In the week before the grand opening, the Smithsonian was all abuzz with a flurry of excitement. Senator Chraft was busy giving a select few of his colleagues an early tour of the ark exhibit. He was doing this because most of them would not be able to attend the opening-night festivities due to prior engagements. He showed them the mural-sized photos of the outside of the ark and also smaller ones of the inside of it as well. He also showed a group photo of Ian, Abu, Hasan, and Aliye outside of the ark, but also using it as a back drop. There were also replicas made of the iron cage doors that were still inside the ark as well as tables and chairs. And also lifelike replicas of animals that were onboard at the time. Clayton explained his lifelong fascination of the ark and about the three men and one woman who found it. There were also areas of the exhibit where hardhats had to be worn because construction was still in progress. After Clayton had spent the week showing the exhibit to his colleagues, it was now time to close it for the grand opening that was going to be taking place that weekend. As he was about to leave the exhibit, the men responsible for it were escorted in by Darrell.

"So, gentlemen, what took you so long to get here?" Clayton asked, looking at Darrell.

"Traffic boss, just because this exhibit is about to open, that doesn't mean traffic is going to change," Darrell said, shrugging his shoulders.

"Fair enough. Gentlemen, let me take you on a quick tour. I think you'll be very impressed," Chraft said, motioning for them to follow him. They saw the mural-sized photo of the picture of the ark that Ian took from the outside and the fiberglass iron bars of the enormous cage that had been painted black from the black hole Aliye guessed must have housed elephants. There was also the replica of the table that Aliye had shot footage of. In the main hall were the life-size statues of Noah and his family with the ark behind them. After the tour was over, Clayton asked if they would either like to say a few words, or just be introduced to the crowd and given credit for their discovery. All of them agreed that it would be better to just be recognized and given credit. Clayton walked the men outside and told them what time to be back the next morning. He explained to them that even though the exhibit would not officially open until the afternoon due to all the press and dignitaries that were going to be there, they still needed to be early so they would be recognized as an official part of the exhibit. They shook hands and parted ways; Clayton turned to face the exhibit one last time before he took his leave. He was mightily impressed and the look on his face reflected that.

CHAPTER 58

"Good afternoon, ladies and gentlemen, distinguished guests, dignitaries, friends, and family members. I want to welcome you all to the Smithsonian Institution's newest exhibit, an exhibit of truly biblical proportions!" Clayton Chraft announced to the crowd standing outside the museum. It was a huge crowd, and one that even the senator himself was impressed by. People lined the streets of the Sant Ocean Hall's Constitution and Tenth Avenue Northwest's location. This museum was a very fitting place to permanently house the Noah's ark exhibit. The hall was a marriage of the Smithsonian's National Museum of Natural History and the National Oceanic and Atmospheric Administration. What better place to have an exhibit dedicated to the global flood of Noah's time but in the hall that is also dedicated to the world's oceans?

Clayton continued his speech.

"Ladies and gentlemen, in just a few minutes, the secretary of this distinguished museum, Dr. Christopher Daniels, and the top two members of the board of regents, Chief Justice Herbert Bostic, Vice President Gerald Anthony, and myself will ceremoniously cut the ribbon to officially open this exhibit. But first, we must take time to recognize three brave men and one woman who was not able to be here, who risked their lives to scale Mount Ararat to search for and find the biblical Noah's ark. Ladies and gentlemen, first I would like to introduce Dr. Ian James, former professor of Egyptology at the University of Oregon. Dr. James was a part of the international studies program there," Clayton said, finishing this part of his speech.

Ian rose to his feet and raised his hands in appreciation of the thunderous applause coming from the huge crowd.

"And to his left, Dr. Abu Mustafa, former curator of the Egyptian Antiquities Museum in Cairo, but in the very near future, he will take his post as the newest curator of the Torquay Museum in Southwest England." Clayton paused as Abu stood and raised his hands as well to also appreciate the crowd's applause. Clayton continued to introduce the last man.

"Last, but most definitely not least, Dr. Hasan Habib. He is an expert in security, heiroglyphics and had helped my office as well as the offices of some of my colleagues on so many occasions. He was a valuable asset on this expedition. Gentlemen, if you please," Clayton said to them and walked over to congratulate them again. They took their seats as he returned to the podium he opened his mouth to speak again when he spotted a familiar face in the crowd. That face belonged to Monty Swanson. He had a look of vileness and anger on his face. Clayton felt sorry for Monty's loss and had told him so before work had begun on the exhibition. Monty told Clayton that if he had an ounce of human dignity, he would not go through with it. Clayton refused, telling Monty that this exhibit was not about him, but an effort to prove the Bible is in fact infallible. Now Monty was there in the crowd to show Clayton his utter contempt for not only this crowd, but this biblical display. Clayton regained his composure and once again began to speak. He saw Monty turn and walk out as he did so.

"Ladies and gentlemen, without further ado, the board of regents and I now cut the ceremonial ribbon and welcome all of you aboard Noah's ark!" Clayton Chraft and the members of the board took their places at the ribbon and with ceremonial scissors cut the ribbon. The applause was deafening as people began to enter the Sant Ocean Hall's museum. The board of regents and Senator Chraft shook each other's hands, and they began to enjoy an afternoon of seeing what life must have been like aboard Noah's ark.

Chapter 59

Later that evening as they walked down Constitution Avenue, the four men talked about that afternoon's activity. Each was extremely impressed with how the exhibit turned out and even more impressed at the large gathering in front of the Sant Ocean Hall. They joked amongst themselves as all of them were still buzzing from all of the excitement.

"I saw Monty Swanson out in the crowd," Clayton confessed to the rest of them.

"When I told him about Tyler and Mahmood, of course he was very distraught, angry, and sad. I told him my heart went out to him and his family. He told me if that were true, I wouldn't have gone through with the ark exhibit," Clayton said, walking with his hands in his pockets and looking at the side walk.

"I wonder how he would have felt had it been us who lost our lives on that mountain instead of Tyler and Mahmood?" Abu asked, finding it hard to care anything about Monty Swanson's loss.

"When a family loses a loved one, that is sad, but when a mad man like Mahmood puts a gun to your face on the sixteen thousand-foot level of a mountain and there is only about forty feet of ledge separating you from another one hundred-foot plunge, I find it hard to care about him," Abu said to Clayton, adding to his comment.

"Well guys, our thoughts and prayers should go out to both Monty and Mahmood's families as well," Chraft said, talking to the men.

They looked at each other and agreed that Clayton was right.

"You know what else I would really like to see on exhibit here in Washington?" Chraft said. Ian and the other two men each looked at each other in complete surprise. They went to Mount Ararat, found the ark, took hundreds of photos of it along with hours of footage inside of it with a blue ray disc recorder, and now there is still something else Clayton would like to see on display in this town.

"What on earth could that possibly be?" Ian asked, almost to shocked to do so.

"Gentlemen, have you ever heard of the Shroud of Turin?" Clayton asked them.

"No, what is that?" Hasan asked. Clayton was more upbeat now, and he walked like a man with his head held high.

"That too, is a biblical artifact. And if you ever get a chance to, read the four gospels, Matthew, Mark, Luke, and John. They describe exactly what it is," he said to them, his voice sounding like they should already know what it is.

They looked at him, wondering if he had now lost his mind.

"Guys, you mean to tell me that you have never heard of the burial cloth of Jesus Christ? Would that not be a most awesome exhibit to be shown in this town?" he said to them, explaining what the shroud was.

"Senator, we don't know that it is the actual burial cloth of Jesus. That has never been proven," Ian replied.

"Semantics, Ian. Purely semantics," Clayton responded.

"Why do is it called the 'Shroud of Turin'?" Hasan asked.

"The shroud is housed in the Royal Chapel of the Cathedral of Saint John in Turin, Italy. Hence, it's name," Clayton informed them.

"Maybe someday soon, it might be brought here. Wouldn't you guys love to see that?" he continued.

The three of them stopped in their tracks and pondered this thought and nodded their heads approvingly at it.

"Who would go and get it?" Abu asked.

"I know of three very well-qualified men who would be most perfect for the job," Clayton answered, walking ahead of them. The three of them each looked at each other as a slight approving look came over their faces.

"Gentlemen, are you coming?" Clayton turned to ask them while he was still walking. Clayton had a huge grin on his face and joy in his heart.

It had been a great day.

ENDNOTES

1. Sarfati, Jonathan. "Noah's Flood and the Gilgamesh Epic." March 29, 2004.www.creationontheweb.com (accessed 2/5/2009).
2. Layard, Austen H. "Inscriptions in the Cuneiform Character from Assyrian Monuments." 1851. www.wikipedia.org (accessed 2/5/2009).
3. "The Church of Jesus Christ of Latter Day Saints." February 12, 2009. www.wikipedia.org (accessed February 12, 2009).
4. "Joseph Smith Jr." February 10, 2009. www.wikipedia.org (accessed February 12, 2009).
5. "Roger Nash Baldwin." January 26, 2009. www.wikipedia.org/wiki/Roger_Nash_Baldwin (accessed March 1, 2009).
6. "Crystal Eastman." August 1, 2008. www.wikipedia.org/wiki/Crystal_Eastman (accessed March 1, 2009).
7. A.J. Muste." February 25, 2009. www.wikipedia.org/wiki/A_J_Muste (accessed March 1, 2009).
8. "Norman Thomas." February 24, 2009. www.wikipedia.org/wiki/Norman_Thomas (accessed March 1, 2009).
9. "Scott Nearing." February 16, 2009. www.wikipedia.org/wiki/Scott_Nearing (accessed March 1, 2009).
10. "Aletta Jacobs." www.alettajacobs.org (accessed March 1, 2009).
11. Hannam, June. "Emmeline Pethick-Lawrence Microsoft Encarta Online Encyclopedia 2008(1997–

2008), http://uk.encarta.msn.com 1997–2008 Microsoft Corporation. (accessed March 1, 2009).
12. "Rosika Schwimmer." February 13, 2009. www.wikipedia.org/wiki/Rosika_Schwimmer (accessed March 1, 2009).
13. "Art Young." December 3, 2008. www.wikipedia.org/wiki/Art_Young (accessed March 1, 2009).
14. "Floyd Dell." 2009.www.answers.com/topic/floyd-dell (accessed March 1, 2009).
15. "Robert Minor." February 23, 2009. www.wikipedia.org/wiki/Robert_Minor (accessed March 1, 2009).
16. "Madelyn Murray O'Hair." January 22, 2009. www.wikipedia.org (accessed February 12, 2009).
17. "Tutankhamun." March 2, 2009. www.wikipedia.org/wiki/Tutankhamun (accessed March 2, 2009).
18. Ganschinetz, Suzanne. "Washington D.C. National Register of Historic Places." (accessed 1/13/2008
19. Ibid.

e|LIVE

listen|imagine|view|experience

AUDIO BOOK DOWNLOAD INCLUDED WITH THIS BOOK!

In your hands you hold a complete digital entertainment package. Besides purchasing the paper version of this book, this book includes a free download of the audio version of this book. Simply use the code listed below when visiting our website. Once downloaded to your computer, you can listen to the book through your computer's speakers, burn it to an audio CD or save the file to your portable music device (such as Apple's popular iPod) and listen on the go!

How to get your free audio book digital download:

1. Visit www.tatepublishing.com and click on the e|LIVE logo on the home page.
2. Enter the following coupon code:
   8cb4-f38f-d1a2-a57a-90d6-3675-2713-bc63
   Download the audio book from your e|LIVE digital locker and begin enjoying your new digital entertainment package today!